Also by James Castagno

Octavia and the Greek Key

Lady of the Lantern

Dance of the Red Panel

Witness to Terror
Fugitive Series Book One

OUT OF TUNIS

Fugitive Series Book Two

James Castagno
A Novella

People seldom do what they believe in. They do what is convenient, then repent.

−Bob Dylan

Chapter I

CLOSE TO HEAVEN

Chasing fugitives across Italy with Carabinieri Captain Angelo Randi provided U.S. Marshals Service Inspector Joe Costa with all the intrigue he needed. A short vacation with his girlfriend, Nina Belsogno, furnished the excitement and the fun.

Seven months had passed since he met Angelo's wife's cousin, Nina. Every detail of their afternoon and evening together that day remained fresh in his mind as if it were yesterday. When the tall blue-gray eyed flight attendant walked into Angelo's office, and pulled her long chestnut hair over her red silk blouse, her beauty caught him by surprise. Angelo said she was pretty, but that understated the facts. Gorgeous, stunning and ravishing didn't seem enough to describe the woman now walking beside him and holding his hand.

A mini vacation with Nina had been hell to plan because of their crazy schedules. The embassy in Rome took four months to give him enough time off and Alitalia Airlines kept her busy flying routes throughout Europe. On top of their scheduling conflicts, the Carabinieri Fugitive Task Force opened five new cases. They kept him and Angelo hustling from Bolzano in the north, to Messina in the south.

"It's amazing you and Angelo went so long without two days off in a row," Nina said.

Joe also could not believe the increased workload. Once he and Angelo had completed testifying before the grand jury in Washington D.C. he figured he'd get a break. Saleh al-Finistini, now in the safe hands of the Witness Security Program, would spend a few years testifying against his former Al Qaeda bosses. He raised his eyebrows and nodded. "If Angelo hadn't convinced Colonel Aldo that he and I needed a break, we'd still be working six days a week."

"How did the colonel know to call Alitalia so I could get a week off from work?"

"He didn't." Joe smiled. "Angelo has a few connections of his own."

Nina furrowed her brow. "What connections?"

"I don't have a clue, but a free week appeared on your schedule at the same time one appeared on mine."

Joe loved two places in Italy. Positano, along the Amalfi coast and the small town of Anacapri at the top of the island of Capri. Nina picked Capri, the closest place to heaven on earth, she called it.

High atop the island, they walked along the sidewalk in front of the Church of San Michele and turned onto Giuseppe Orlandi Street. Joe squeezed Nina's hand, and they headed toward the Galleria della'Arte ceramic shop. *How did I get so lucky? A flight attendant who looks like a movie star, and a member of my partner's family.*

Nina stopped, tilted her head and raised her eyebrows. "I've been meaning to ask you what happened to the terrorist the Carabinieri arrested. Is that why you and Angelo went to America?"

"Yeah, we took him there, but back then I couldn't say anything to you. Italian and American authorities are now hauling him around the world to be interviewed by terrorism investigators."

"He didn't go to jail?"

Joe smiled and winked. "Not yet, but he will."

Nina pursed her lips. "Hope it's for the rest of his life."

"Not likely, even though he killed forty children. That guy provided more information on Al Qaeda than anyone else ever has. He'll spend time in prison, but it won't be hard time." Joe raised her hand and kissed it. "Let's not talk about work. Tell me about your new apartment."

"It's a two bedroom. You'll like it."

"How do you know?"

"The embassy is a twenty-minute walk."

"Love it already, but that's an expensive area of town."

"We have a new flight attendant, Monique LaCroix. She's Algerian... French father. We'll share it."

"Is she new on the job?"

"New to Alitalia. She flew for Air Arabia out of Alexandria, Egypt, but wanted to work in the EU. Someone told me they hired her because she speaks five languages."

"Are you sure she'll be a good roommate?"

"Yes, but I don't plan to introduce you to her for a while." She poked him in the rips. "She's exceedingly beautiful."

Joe wrapped his arms around her. "There is only one exceedingly beautiful woman on earth, I'm holding her in my arms." He stepped back. "Come, it's our last night here. The day after tomorrow we'll both be back to work, and busy as hell."

"I don't think it's possible to work more than you did for the past few months."

"Tracking fugitives is not an eight-to-five job."

Chapter II

THE IRAN IRIS

The rusted 270 foot cargo ship, MV *Iran Iris*, had plied the ports along the Mediterranean coast for the past ten years. *Busy cargo vessels don't look like cruise ships, but this rust bucket is long overdue a new paint-job,* Omar Hassan thought.

He felt out of place standing on the bridge scanning the horizon with field glasses. His black dress pants and dark blue silk shirt identified him as an outsider. He wasn't fond of ships and had never thought of working on one. The three-man bridge crew wore white. *Moving cargo... a dirty job. Why white uniforms?*

He lowered the binoculars and looked at Captain Jamal Jalili, his soiled white shirt a size too small for his large frame, and protruding belly. The man barely fit in the captain's chair and looked to be a physical wreck, but he had never missed a voyage. *Why would he? His cut from the delivery of twenty-five kilos of heroin exceeded most Tunisian's yearly pay.*

Omar looked through the field glasses and contemplated the last year. This was his fifth trip on the rusted freighter and the one voyage that bothered him the most. Transferring heroin to the mafia and collecting the payment was easy. Murder wasn't.

Thirty minutes earlier, Omar positioned four men along the side of the cargo deck. They taped dark plastic on the open steel railing to conceal themselves from any vessel pulling alongside the ship. Two of them held AK47 rifles, the other two held RPG-7 Rocket-Propelled Grenade Launchers. A black backpack, containing a kilo of C4 plastic explosive, lay at their feet.

A young woman in a torn, food-stained sundress, slouched as she carried bottles of water through the door near the captain's chair. The girl lowered her gaze when Omar looked at her black eye and bruised cheek.

Jamal spun his chair toward her. "What are you doing here? I told you to stay in the galley."

She set the bottles on the floor and scurried out the door.

The women back in Tunisia won't come near this bastard. He recalled the girl was brought aboard the *Iran Iris* almost a year ago. She had kept him company a few times, but after the captain had his way with her, there wasn't much left to look at. "You treat her too nice," Omar said.

Captain Jalili stood and kicked the plastic water bottles across the deck. He turned piercing eyes to Omar indicating the remark didn't sit well with him. "This is my vessel, I do what I want." He pointed at Omar. "Worry about what you must do. How did Majid find out his new customer was the Italian police?"

Careful. He's worked for Majid longer than I have. If he throws me overboard, it will take one day for Majid to hire my replacement. "We don't know. He has an informant in Rome. The guy must be a police officer or someone who works for them. He told Majid everything about their plan, even the name of the fishing boat."

"Be with your men when they come alongside and do it quickly. I want to be on the other side of Crete when the Italians come looking for revenge."

Omar nodded and raised the binoculars. "They're coming." He bolted from the bridge.

###

Five undercover officers, dressed in old clothes purchased on the docks of Naples, manned the fishing boat. Italian Narcotics Officer Paolo Borelli and DEA Agent Ralph Marino led the deck crew of three other agents, one American and two Italian. They had worked the case together for the past six months. *Three million dollars' worth of heroin will never make it to the streets of New York City,* thought Ralph.

The forty-foot trawler, San Giovanni, out of the port of Naples, appeared to be a fishing vessel. The boat's one oddity was the twin marine radar domes above the wheelhouse. One, a compact global maritime terminal, provided simultaneous data and voice communication with the Carabinieri Counter-Narcotics Group, monitoring from Naples.

Paolo kept his eyes on the cargo ship a quarter mile in front of the trawler and leaned out a window. "Get ready!"

One of the Italian officers moved to the bow and the other two men ran to the stern.

During the briefing on the dock in Naples, Paolo stressed to his men they needed to get a good look at everyone lowering the drugs from the ship. He wanted each officer to identify them when they were arrested and taken to court. He took one hand off the wheel and reached for a toggle switch. "I'm turning on the microphones, they'll hear everything at headquarters."

Ralph raised a set of binoculars and focused on the railing of the MV *Iran Iris'* cargo deck. "The informant was right. Hassan is standing next to the railing." He lowered the field glasses. "How long will the transfer take?"

"Once alongside, ten minutes. I want to get the drugs and give them the money as fast as possible." Paolo pointed at a hand-held spotlight. "Signal them now."

Omar leaned on the cargo deck railing. His four men squatted behind the plastic, their weapons ready. "I'll tell you when to shoot."

The trawler slowed and began its turn to position itself parallel with the ship.

"Not yet. Wait... wait," Omar said.

The smaller vessel pull alongside and bounce off the hull of *Iran Iris*. "Now!" he said.

The four men stood and the two with AK-47's opened fire. The other two leaned over the railing and aimed their RPG-7's at the wheelhouse and the aft deck.

Bullets raked across the deck and into the roof of the trawler's wheelhouse. The Italian officer at the bow dove to a folded canvas tarp lying on the deck and pulled a Spectre M4 submachine gun from beneath it. He raised the weapon as bullets slammed into his body.

Omar clamped both his hands over his ears and ducked to the deck as one man fired his RPG-7 into the trawler. The second rocket exploded an instant later.

He picked up the backpack, cradled it under his arm and yanked the cap from the pull-wire fuse lighter. He threw it over the side and watched it bounce on the deck below the fishing boats wheelhouse. From his pocket he yanked a hand-held radio. "Get away from them, fast."

The deck vibrated as the propeller turned and the ship pulled away from the trawler. When they were a hundred meters from the small vessel, the charge exploded sending parts of the boat into the air.

Omar cringed as the burning boat listed to one side and disappear below the surface. *Murder isn't easy, even when it's necessary.*

Chapter III

FIND HIM

The evening of their last day on island of Capri, Joe and Nina had caught the tail end of a news broadcast about the deaths of the five narcotics officers. He held back his eagerness to call Angelo, knowing a more detailed account of what happened would mar their vacation with bad news.

For the next week back in Rome, Joe kept up with the Italian press stories of the murders. Every newspaper in Italy ran daily updates on their front page. Higher-ups at the Carabinieri Counter-Narcotics Group struggled to answer questions from the press without releasing sensitive case information. The Drug Enforcement Administration sent the Special Agent-In-Charge of the Washington D.C. office to Rome to coordinate the investigation with the Department of Justice.

Joe realized the Fugitive Task Force would get a call, and he waited for his partner, to notify him when it did. It came on a Friday morning and by ten o'clock he sat at a table in a conference room next to Carabinieri Colonel Aldo's large office. He hadn't seen the colonel since he and Angelo returned from Washington.

Seated next to him were Angelo, and Lieutenant Sergio Lacona. Joe wore a dark suit and the Carabinieri officers wore their distinctive dark uniforms. A leather briefcase sat on the floor beside Sergio.

Colonel Aldo stepped into the room and closed the door. All three men stood. Aldo motioned them to sit and lowered his imposing frame into the chair at the head of the table. He looked at Lieutenant Lacona. "Did you bring the reports, Sergio?"

"Yes, sir." He raised his briefcase and slid it onto the table.

Angelo glanced at the colonel and looked at Joe. He pressed his lips together and raised his eyebrows.

Joe eyed Sergio as he opened the briefcase. It was the first time the young lieutenant had carried it to one of Aldo's meetings. *Scratch the colonel's table, and he'll chew you a new asshole.*

Sergio looked at Colonel Aldo the instant he pointed at the briefcase and frowned. He lifted it, placed it on his lap, and removed two thick folders. Before he set them on the table he glanced at Aldo, who was now smiling. "This is all the information in our files on Omar Hassan and his boss Majid Ziyad. Six months ago our informant identified Hassan. A Rome judge issued the warrant for his arrest. We haven't been able to find him, but if the ship stops in a European Union port, we'll get him."

"Is there an open fugitive case on Hassan?" Aldo asked Angelo.

"Yes, sir, but we haven't been working it. We didn't want to interfere with the Narcotics Group and the American DEA undercover operation."

Sergio leaned forward and looked at the colonel. "Hassan is not his real name."

Aldo nodded. "Where is he now?"

Angelo shrugged. "We know he was on the ship. After Agent Borelli turned on the microphones, you can hear DEA Agent Marino say Omar was standing on deck. After that, little except for automatic weapons fire and an explosion is heard. If he's not still there, then he's back in Tunisia."

"How is Ziyad involved?"

Sergio pointed at the folders in front of Aldo. "It's explained in the case file, sir. Majid Ziyad owns and operates MZ Shipping and Export. He supplies cheap products to thousands of small stores throughout the Mediterranean and Europe. During the past five years, he's been bringing in heroin from Afghanistan. The men who work for him moving the drugs have been hard to identify. They don't use their real names."

Aldo furrowed his brow and bit his lower lip. "Is there's an arrest warrant for Ziyad?"

"No, Sir. There isn't enough information to satisfy a judge."

Aldo nodded and looked at Angelo. "Were you told about the trawler operation?"

"Yes, sir. Because of the Fugitive Task Force case on Omar."

"Did your DEA tell you about it, Inspector Costa?"

"Yes, sir, but it was only a passing comment, no specific details."

Aldo paused, pressed his palms together, and placed his fingertips against his chin. "How did Ziyad and Hassan find out police were on the trawler?" he asked Lieutenant Lacona.

Sergio shook his head. "We're not sure. Only ten people had knowledge of the operation. Someone here in Rome is giving them information."

Aldo pointed at Captain Randi. "Start today Angelo. Interview the other nine people. Since two of the men killed were American, have Inspector Costa hand carry my official request to the ambassador. My secretary will have it ready for you in an hour. Where's the ship?"

Joe answered when the others remained silent. "Somewhere in the Med, sir. The U.S. Navy has offered to help find it."

Aldo paused and rubbed the stubble on his cheek. "Good, ask them to start." He looked at Angelo. "It's been many years since three Carabinieri were killed on the same day, and the first time American agents died while assisting Italy. Find Hassan. Make it your top priority. I want the bastard brought to Rome."

Chapter IV

MONIQUE

Monique LaCroix had met Omar Hassan while on vacation at Sharm el-Sheikh on the southern tip of the Sinai Peninsula.

During that evening she glanced at him twice and he slipped her a business card while she sat at the nightclub bar in the five star Cleopatra Luxury Resort. From that night on, their relationship flourished.

Six months later, she and Omar finished their lunch in a restaurant overlooking the water along Rue du Lac Biwa in Tunis. "Do you think the Italians will find out who did it?" she asked.

Omar shook his head. "No, they had no idea we knew the police were on the fishing boat."

She toyed with an intricate gold bracelet, spinning it around her wrist. "This is beautiful. Where did you get it?"

"At the souk el Birka... the former slave market which closed four hundred years ago. The best gold shops in Tunis are there."

"Thank you." She kissed him. "Your boss must be rich and pay well."

"I'm Majid's most trusted man."

Monique furrowed her brow. "Majid? Didn't you tell me you worked for a man named Ziyad?"

He pressed his lips together and raised his eyebrows. "His first name is Majid, but tell no one I work for his company at the port. It's best not to talk about my employment."

"I won't." She held a hand in front of a passing waiter. "Excuse me. Please take our photo," she said handing him her cell phone. As she leaned against Omar, she raised the bracelet.

The waiter snapped the picture, smiled at Omar and returned the phone.

Omar's cell phone rang, and he tapped the screen to end the call.

"Was that your wife?"

He nodded.

"Will you stay with me tonight?" she asked.

"I would if it was possible. Your overnight flights give me little time to plan. We'll be together for a while but she expects me to return."

Monique never had a boyfriend as generous as Omar. She hated sharing him with a wife. *I wish he'd end that marriage.* "When are you going to leave her?"

"You and I have been together only six months. I need to plan everything. You want to be happy don't you?"

"Yes, but I don't want to be number two."

He placed a hand over hers. "Don't worry, we'll be together soon and I'll have enough money to start a new life. How do you like working for Alitalia?"

Monique shrugged. "Most of the large airlines are the same. There's less turmoil in Italy than in Egypt."

Omar smiled. "And the food is much better." He removed an envelope from a pocket and handed it to her. "When you get back to Rome, buy a stamp and mail this for me. Don't open it."

The next day Nina, wearing a bathrobe, relaxed on the couch in her apartment and watched television. Packed and half-full boxes lay near a hallway leading to the bedrooms. The deadbolt clicked open and Monique entered dragging her overnight bag.

Nina sat up. "How was your trip?"

Monique sashayed across the room and extended her arm, showing off the bracelet. "Wonderful. Did you get the picture I sent?"

"Yes, let me see."

Monique raised her wrist. "Omar bought it before I arrived."

Nina rubbed a finger across the chain. Her eyes widened. "Beautiful."

"Next time come with me, you'll like him."

She sighed. "If we ever get on the same schedule I might. My flight leaves tonight."

Monique pulled her bag to her bedroom and returned. "I'm hungry, want to get something to eat?"

Nina slid from the couch. "Wish I could but I need to get ready, maybe tomorrow," she said heading to her bedroom.

"I'm going to get a pizza, I'll see you when you get back," Monique yelled from the living room.

Five minutes later Nina walked out of the bedroom in her bra and uniform skirt. *Damn, I hope she has a clean work blouse I can borrow.* She went into Monique's room, stepped to the closet and removed a white shirt from a hanger. As she turned, she knocked a book off the nightstand and a folded newspaper article fell to the floor. When she picked them up, she read the headline 'Murdered Police' at the top of the article, and 'Diary' embossed on the front of the book. She set the book on the night stand and slid the article back into the diary. *Why does she keep an article about that?*

The next afternoon, Nina sat in an empty car on the Leonardo Express train heading from the airport to the train terminal in central Rome. *Joe won't mind if I call him at work.* She pulled out her cell phone and hit the speaker icon.

"How is my Roman lover today... you back?" Joe asked.

"Yes and she better be your only lover."

"No one else stands a chance."

"Will you take me to dinner tonight?"

"I'd love to, what time?"

"Nine. I'm still unpacking boxes."

"Your roommate home?"

"No."

"Good. I'll be there at eight-thirty for a few kisses before we leave."

She laughed. "Come at eight and I'll show you how I'm decorating my bedroom."

Later that evening Joe and Nina sat in the back of the Ciao Bella restaurant, not far from the U.S. Embassy. The waiter cleared their empty plates and filled their wine glasses from a bottle on the table.

"When do you want me to help move the old couch and chair out of your apartment?" Joe asked.

"Oh, I forgot to tell you about the new furniture. I took pictures." She slid her phone across the table. "The photos are on the phone... it's the tan leather couch and chair." Nina stood. "I'm going to the bathroom. I'll only be a minute."

Joe picked up her phone and smiled as she scooted between tables and disappear down a hallway. He tapped the screen and scanned the pictures until he came to a photo of the couch. Next were two pictures from different angles followed by a close-up of an oversized chair. He went to the next picture and stopped breathing when the image appeared. *What the hell is this?* An attractive woman, holding her arm up and pointing at a large gold bracelet, sat beside a fugitive he and Angelo wanted to arrest.

He frowned, put the phone on table and looked to the hallway just as Nina stepped into the room. As she drew near, he tapped the chair beside him. "Sit next to me."

She took a seat and edged the chair closer to his. "Did you like the furniture?"

Joe stared into her eyes. "Yes."

Nina raised her eyebrows. "What's wrong? You look mad."

"No, not mad, worried." He picked up her cell phone, swiped a finger across the screen and turned it toward her. "Where did you get this photo?"

Nina grabbed the phone. "What's the matter with you? That's my roommate Monique and her boyfriend."

Joe's heart pounded as he took her hand. "Please listen. This is important. Did you take the picture?"

Nina pulled her hand from his. "What's wrong? Why are you staring at me? Monique emailed it from Tunisia."

"I'm sorry if I scared you." He looked away and paused. "Have you met him?"

Nina turned her chair toward him. "Quit acting like a cop interrogating a criminal. You're frightening me. Tell me why you're concerned."

Joe raised his hand and touched her cheek. "There's a possibility you could be in danger."

Nina stiffened. "Me?"

Joe looked into her eyes and nodded. "Remember on Capri we heard about the drug agents killed during the undercover operation?"

"Yes."

"I recognize the man in the photo. He's the one who killed them."

Nina's eyes widened and her mouth dropped open. Her eyes darted from side to side. "That can't be. Monique told me she's been going out with him for six months."

"Omar. That's his name, isn't it?"

Nina took a deep breath. "How did you know?"

Joe took both her hands in his. "Angelo and I are looking for him, he's a fugitive. Email me the photo. Let's go back to my apartment. We need to talk before I see Angelo."

Chapter V

THE NOTES

Angelo faced a two-drawer safe against the wall behind his desk. He slid the top drawer shut and turned the combination dial.

Mia, not only his secretary, but his wife Sofia's cousin, tapped on the doorframe. "Joe is here to see you."

"Send him in."

Joe strode into the room, pulled a chair to the front of the desk and took a seat. "You busy?"

"No." He raised a finger and looked toward the door. "Mia bring us coffee!"

Joe took a deep breath and exhaled. "Something came up... you need to hear this."

"Are you and Nina okay?"

"Couldn't be better."

"What is it?"

Joe opened the photo of Monique and Omar on his phone. "Take a look at this." He handed it to Angelo.

Angelo's mouth fell open. "Jesus, that's Hassan!" He didn't blink as he stared at the picture for five seconds. "Where the hell did you get this?"

Joe raised his eyebrows and cocked his head. "I had dinner with Nina last night." He pointed at his phone. "That photo is on her phone."

Angelo leaned over his desk. "What the hell... Nina's phone?"

"The girl next to Omar is Monique LaCroix. She's Nina's new roommate and Hassan's girlfriend."

Angelo paused and stared at him. "Monique who? Roommate? Nina knows Omar Hassan?"

"Thank God, no. They've never met. In the photo the roommate is having lunch with him in Tunis, and he gave her the bracelet. She sent Nina the photo."

"Did Nina know we're looking for him?"

"Come on Angelo. Until last night she didn't. When I saw the picture, I almost fell out of my chair. I explained everything to her but that's not all of it. Nina found a newspaper article about the murdered drug agents in Monique's room."

Angelo shook his head and pulled a notepad from his desk drawer. "Let's go back over everything you said."

An hour later, Angelo shoved the pad aside and rubbed his temple. "Did you tell anyone else?"

"No. Once I explained to Nina about Omar, she said she'd try to find more information. She mentioned a diary in the room, but when I suggested she read it, she refused. You and I would read it but I guess women take their diaries serious. I told her to stay out of Monique's belongings for the moment."

"Were you introduced to her roommate?"

"Hell, no. Ever since the Milan court convicted the CIA agents, most Italians are cautious with people working at the U.S. Embassy. An American cop working in Italy may raise a few questions. Nina even told me no one at Alitalia knows there's a Carabinieri Captain in the family. I want her name kept out of it."

Angelo tapped his notes. "I must tell Colonel Aldo."

"I want her identity protected, Angelo. She's a member of your family and she's important to me."

Angelo pressed his palms together and placed his fingertips against his lips. He did not move for ten seconds, lowered his hands and lifted his head. "Her name can be kept secret. We need to put this information in a report and bury these pages and the photo. We'll give her a code name. What are you doing for the rest of the day?"

Joe sat up in the chair. "Drinking a lot of coffee and helping you write the perfect report."

After Angelo and Joe left the office, a man in gray work clothes shuffled into Angelo's office. He walked to the desk, removed papers from the center drawer, and grinned. *Keep leaving it open for me.* He took less than two minutes to make notes and replace the pages in the drawer.

Early the next morning, Joe and Angelo rushed into Colonel Aldo's conference room. Sergio, Paul Sacca, the embassy's resident DEA Special Agent, and the Colonel sat at the table. Aldo occupied his customary position at one end.

They both sat and Joe set a file folder on the table.

Angelo took a deep breath and looked at his boss. "Sorry we requested this quick meeting and were late. It concerns the agents murdered on the trawler."

Joe placed a hand on the file. "We have an informant who has asked to remain confidential... we gave him the code name Miami." He handed a copy of their investigative report to Aldo and slid copies to the others. He and Angelo waited for everyone to read the report.

"Sir. We need your permission to keep this person's name secret," Angelo said. "For now, only Joe and I will know the true identity."

Aldo cocked his head to the side. "Odd request, Captain Randi."

Angelo nodded and his eyes pled his case.

"Tell us more."

"Our informant, Miami, knows Omar Hassan's girlfriend... who happens to live in Rome."

"How's that? Are they friends?" Paul asked.

Joe glanced at Angelo. The report they wrote provided no information about their informant and they hadn't planned on answering questions. "They've gone out together," Joe said.

Sergio raised his eyebrows. "Does Hassan realize his girlfriend is cheating on him?"

"No," Joe said.

The colonel furrowed his brow. "What is the girlfriend's name?"

Angelo turned a sheepish look to him. "If possible, we also want to keep her name secret."

Joe held his breath. *He may not want to approve it.* He needed to convince him to agree with their out of the ordinary appeal. Nina's life depended on it. Joe interrupted. "Sir, Miami refuses to talk to us if the girlfriend is followed or questioned. Lives depend on this."

Aldo studied Joe for a second. "If I agree Inspector Costa, understand, the Italian government will one day demand a name."

"If this helps us capture Hassan, once we get our hands on him, we'll release the name," Angelo said. "I talked to everyone briefed on the operation and still have no idea how Omar and Majid are getting information. If we name the informant and girlfriend now, there's a chance someone will get killed."

Aldo leaned back in his chair, scanned the walls and turned to Angelo. "No leads at all?"

"Not yet, sir, but I'm working on it."

Joe could almost see the wheels turning inside Aldo's head as he took a minute to reread the two-page report.

He dropped the pages in front of him, leaned on the table and looked at Angelo. "Let me think about your request. I'll call you in two hours. What is being done about Hassan's Sicilian drug connection, Nari Saladino?"

Sergio smiled. "He's in Rome, we're picking him up tomorrow night."

When Joe left the meeting he returned to the embassy. As he walked toward the entrance, FBI Agent Robert Duffy called his name and ran up to him. "I heard you went to a meeting about the trawler case."

"Yeah, with Colonel Aldo."

Duffy shuffled his feet. "No one told me about it."

Joe tilted his head to the side. "Damn, didn't someone on Aldo's staff call you?"

"No, and FBI headquarters won't like being shoved aside. They may have the Justice Department put pressure on people."

Joe raised his eyebrows. "Reconsider before you start something. Colonel Aldo is not someone you want to give agita... you know what that means?"

"No."

"Heartburn. If people make demands, he'll go to the Minister. The Italians will cut the FBI out of the case, and you'll watch this investigation through a telescope."

"Two Americans died on that trawler," Duffy said.

"And three Italians. The Italian government will not roll over because the Bureau throws a tantrum. Play it cool. I'll talk to Captain Randi and see if I can get the ball rolling. I'm sure it's an oversight. DEA is already involved." Joe tapped Duffy on the shoulder. "I'll mention it to the colonel." He headed to his office.

The colonel and Angelo considered Duffy too inexperienced for the position he held at the embassy. The last thing Joe wanted to do was to voice his opinion. *No dog in that fight.*

Chapter VI

MAJID

Majid Ziyad smiled. He had done well for himself. At forty-five, he owned an export business in Tunis that sent goods to stores throughout the Mediterranean and Europe. Shipments went out once a month on the MV *Iran Iris*. He sat behind the executive desk in a large office furnished with a leather couch, chairs and a carved wooden coffee table. When Omar walked into the office, he closed the folder on the desk and motioned to a chair.

Omar took a seat and Majid moved to the couch.

"Did you give her the letter?" Majid asked.

Omar nodded. "She'll mail it from Rome."

"We'll see if it arrives."

"It will. I told you she's trustworthy."

Majid smiled. "Will she agree to move half-kilo size shipments when she flies to Italy?"

"I didn't bring it up yet. She didn't ask any questions about the letter. I don't think there will be a problem."

"Are you paying her?"

"Just expensive gifts."

"Be careful what you say. While she's in Italy we have no control. The more she knows the more dangerous it is to our operation. I wouldn't want to ask you to kill her."

"She'll say nothing, she likes what I give her."

Majid shook his head. "What about your wife?"

Omar raised his eyebrows. "She better never find out."

Majid stood, indicating the end of their conversation. "Call Nari. Tell him the next shipment is on time."

Omar left and closed the door.

He returned to the desk and tapped the screen of his cell phone.

"How is your mother?" Majid asked. He nodded and smiled. "Good. The more information you get, the more money you'll make."

As he listened to the man, his eyes widened. "Nari? When?"

He pushed the chair back and stood. "Tomorrow night?" He furrowed his brow and glanced across the room. "Thank you. I'll send an extra payment... double the money."

Majid ended the call and stared at his desktop. He tapped the cell phone and dropped into the chair.

Nari answered. "Hello."

"How are you today?"

"Good. Is there a problem?"

The last thing Majid wanted to do was make his Italian drug connection nervous. "No. I want to be sure your distributors are ready."

"They are. I talked to each of them."

"Fine. Did the letter arrive?"

"Yes."

Good, she passed the test. "Okay. I'll call before the shipment leaves." Majid hung up, made another call and waited for an answer. "Yassine, it's me. I have a job for you."

Chapter VII

THE ARREST

At ten the next night a police car and a van occupied the corner of a secured parking area outside the Carabinieri Counter-Narcotics Group. Angelo and Joe stood beside an Alfa Romeo parked ten meters away from Lieutenant Sergio Lacona, and four of his men dressed in dark tactical uniforms.

"We'll follow them," Angelo said. "It's their case and they don't want us getting in the way. When we get to the club, stay in the car until they grab him."

"No problem. You think he knows about the freighter?"

"He's getting most of his heroin from Majid. I'm sure he does and I plan to squeeze the information out of him."

###

Two miles from Vatican City, a crowd and a fifty foot long line formed along the sidewalk outside a nightclub. Classic rock blasted from a speaker above the closed double doors. Motorcycles and scooters lined the opposite curb along the narrow street.

Yassine, a dark-skinned man in his twenties, with a close-cropped beard, stood in line ten people behind Nari Saladino, and his much too young date. Yassine smiled at her high heels, skin-tight low-cut jeans and an undersized vest battling to retain her ample breasts. He glanced at a kid sitting on his scooter across the street and nodded.

Nari's cell phone rang. He lifted a hand to his date and stepped into the street to answer it.

The boy on the scooter raised his eyebrows and nodded to Yassine as he started the engine, pulled away from the curb, and stopped. "Hi Nari," he yelled.

Nari looked up, squinted at him and half waved as the scooter headed up the street.

Yassine glanced in both directions. He wiped his perspiring right hand against his pants leg. Prior to stepping into the street, he turned to the girls behind him, held up a finger, and nodded. As he walked up behind Nari, he pulled a pistol from his pocket, and fired one shot into the back of the drug dealer's head.

The crowd panicked, women screamed and people shoved each other to back away from the curb. The girls he had motioned to shrieked, spun around and raced down the street. Yassine took off in the same direction, jumping over a couple who had fallen in the street. He fled with the crowd and bolted down an intersecting alley.

Angelo's Alfa Romeo followed the speeding van and marked police car to the front of the nightclub. He slammed on the brakes, skidded to a stop and jumped out.

What the hell happened? Joe threw open the passenger side door and ran to Angelo's side. "No sense in sitting in the car. It ended before we arrived."

Sergio and his men, carrying Spectre M4 submachine guns, secured the area near the body, and in front of the club.

Angelo and Joe stepped beside Sergio, standing next to Saladino's body.

"Looks as if he pissed off the wrong people, or someone found out you were coming." Joe said to Sergio.

The next morning, Angelo, with an empty feeling in the pit of his stomach, walked to Colonel Aldo's office. Joe called earlier and said he didn't want to stick his nose into Carabinieri affairs. He would have been more comfortable with Joe at his side.

Angelo marched to the front of Aldo's desk and came to attention.

"Sit down Captain Randi."

Normally it's Angelo... not good. "Good morning, sir."

"Sit."

He dropped into a straight-back chair in front of the desk and pressed himself against the thin wood slats.

"It wasn't your operation, but what happened last night?"

"We were two blocks away when we heard the call. He was dead before we arrived."

Aldo shook his head. "The Commanding General wants answers. He's been on the phone with the Minister who is mad as hell. He's ready to replace people in the Narcotics Group, and we're not far down the line."

Angelo held his breath a moment. "Sir, somebody is getting information, and whoever it is, they're related to the trawler case. As far as I know the Narcotics Group decided to pick up Saladino weeks ago. After he arrived in Rome, they chose the day."

"I assume the same people briefed on the trawler case knew of Saladino's imminent arrest?"

"I believe so."

"And you interviewed each of them?"

Angelo nodded. "Yes, sir."

"The Americans?"

"The Ambassador allowed Joe and me to speak with them. Their embassy has security standards that meet or exceed ours."

Aldo leaned over his desk. "Two outside investigators will look into the matter. Prepare yourself for questions. I suggest you have the right answers." He picked up a folder on his desk.

The colonel had finished. He headed to the door, and when Aldo called his name he stopped and turned. "Yes, sir?"

"Miami's name stays secret. If I were you I wouldn't bring up your informant. Answer their questions, but get them off our asses."

Chapter VIII

THE INVITATION

Nina shook her head as she pulled her suitcase down the passageway leading from the plane. She looked at her white tennis shoes, "Damn it". Nothing went right since she met with the other flight attendants at the Munich airport. The heel of a shoe broke off getting on the plane and the flight into Rome had no vacant seats. Rowdy passengers returning from a Roma and Bayern Munich soccer game filled the cabin. Roma won the game and their followers continued to party on the flight home. When she stepped into the gate waiting area, Joe and Angelo waved to her.

"Hi beautiful," Joe said as he kissed her.

Angelo kissed her cheeks. "Tired?"

"I am."

"Sneakers? Where are your heels?" Joe asked.

"Don't ask, it's been a bad day."

Joe took her bag and hand. "Angelo thought it would be nice to pick you up in the Alfa."

Joe met her at the airport whenever he had time, but she hadn't told him which flight she planned to take. It seemed odd Angelo was with him. "Is everything all right? How did you know my flight number?"

"A family member, who works in the tower, made a few calls," Angelo said.

Nina grinned. *Got more connections than a hooker with a little black book.* "Your cousin, or my cousin on your wife's side?"

He smiled. "A Randi."

Angelo and Joe sat in the two large chairs near the coffee table. Nina, who had been talking to her cousin, walked into the office.

Angelo gave her his seat and dropped onto the couch. "Joe said you don't have a telephone in the apartment."

"Just cell phones."

"What's Monique's number?" Joe asked.

"336, 811, 2114."

Angelo wrote the number on a note pad. "Does she use email?"

"Yes, tiscali... LaCroix, a period, and Monique."

"Does she email Omar?" Joe asked.

"I don't know."

Joe slid to the edge of his chair and leaned toward her. "If you don't want to, you don't have to do this. Try to get her to talk... tell her something made you angry."

"It won't be difficult, I'm already mad at her."

"We may want to put a microphone in her room. For now, talk to her and keep good notes. Don't hunt for more information in her room. She may notice things misplaced and I don't want her to get suspicious." Angelo said.

"Okay, anything else?"

"Yeah," Joe said. "Keep it simple. The more complicated the story you make up, the harder it will be remembering it. Let's get coffee and I'll get a taxi for you."

"I have a call to make. Meet you at the bakery down the street," Angelo said.

Joe, drinking espresso, sat alone in the bakery when Angelo arrived. "She left a few minutes ago."

Angelo walked to the counter, got a coffee and returned. "I'm sure the informant is inside the Narcotics Group Headquarters."

"Thank Jesus we didn't give anyone Nina's name," Joe said.

Angelo downed his espresso and slid away from the table. "Let's go back to my office and develop a plan."

Nina walked into her apartment and saw Monique on the couch half asleep. She left her bag by the door. "Hi."

"I thought you'd be home earlier."

"The police were on the train from the airport. A woman stole a purse, and they said I looked like her." She dropped onto the couch.

Monique shook her head and frowned. "Don't they have better things to do? They could chase politicians who steal millions of Euros."

Nina took advantage of the opportunity, raised her head and smiled. "Chase politicians? Why? No one wants to lose their job or the money that changes hands."

"They're useless. When's your next flight?"

"I'm off for three days. You?"

"Me too. Want to meet Omar? We can fly to Tunis tomorrow."

Meet a killer? "I don't know. He'll want to be alone with you."

"I'll call him and ask." She leapt from the couch and dashed to her bedroom.

Nina sat on the couch and gazed around the room. *It might help Joe if I go.* She pressed her lips together and frowned. Concerned with her safety whenever she traveled, he always reminded her to lock her door, watch her bags, and guard her purse. Going to Tunis wouldn't set well with him and once she told him she planned to meet Omar, he'd go crazy. *Better find an excuse.* She lifted the television remote and clicked through channels.

Monique ran from the hallway. "He wants us to come and said we can stay in the villa."

"What villa?"

"His boss Majid owns it. It's on the outskirts of Tunis."

"I don't know. You sure it's no problem if I go?"

"Of course not. You'll have fun... we'll stay one night."

She answered without thinking of the ramifications. "Okay, make the flight arrangements."

"Great, I'll shower... let's go shopping."

"I'll take one when you're finished," Nina said as Monique headed down the hall.

She walked to her bedroom, closed the door and called Joe's cell phone. Two taps on the screen lowered the speaker volume. *Why did I say yes?*

"Embassy, Costa."

"Hi Joe." There was a pause.

"You home?"

"Yes."

"Is something wrong?"

"No but I need to tell you something. Don't be mad."

"Nothing you can do to make me angry."

"Good. I'm going to Tunis with Monique."

"You're what?"

"It's a chance to meet Omar... just for one night." She looked at the phone waiting for a response.

"No. You can't."

"Monique came up with the idea. I'll get more information. It will help you capture him."

"It's too dangerous."

"Why?"

"It just is."

"I've decided to go!"

"Nina, please."

"No." She heard him sigh.

"When do you leave?"

"Tomorrow morning."

"I want to see you before you go."

So he can change my mind. "I won't have time... it's only for one night."

"Okay. Keep your cell phone with you and call as soon as you get back."

"I will, don't worry."

"Worry? I'll go nuts while you're gone."

"I'll make it up to you when I get home. I love you."

"I love you more."

Joe wasted no time. He called Angelo and asked him not to leave his office until they spoke.

Outside the door in front of Mia's office, he stopped. *Why won't Nina listen?* Trying to change her mind was fruitless. Although it wouldn't make him feel much better, he knew she'd be cautious. She often told him her degree in psychology taught her to spend more time listening and less talking. *Love her attitude but getting involved in a major international investigation isn't a smart decision. Angelo won't like this.*

Before Mia looked up from her keyboard he stepped past her and marched into Angelo's office.

Angelo, flipping through a file on his desk, didn't see him enter.

"Glad you're sitting. You don't want to be standing when you hear this."

Angelo smiled. "Relax. Whatever you say can't be any more of a surprise than the photo on Nina's phone." He shoved a stack of papers aside, looked at Joe and furrowed his brow. "Something bothering you?"

"That word isn't strong enough and angry only approaches the way I feel." He dragged a chair in front of the desk and dropped into it. "You will not believe this. Your wife's cousin... my girlfriend... is going to Tunis with her roommate."

Angelo took a deep breath, his eyes widened. "Tell me they're only going shopping."

Joe glanced at the floor. "Monique's going to introduce her to Omar."

Angelo bolted upright in his chair. "Is she crazy?"

"I asked, and she wasn't happy about it."

"Tell her not to go."

Joe took a deep breath and shook his head. "You've known her longer than I. Ever been able to tell her what to do?"

Angelo held a finger in front of his lips, lowered his hand and looked toward the office door. "Mia! Shut my door and don't disturb us." He waited until it closed and lowered his voice. "Once she makes a decision, that's it. If Mia or my wife find out they'll blame us, no matter what Nina says. When is she supposed to leave?"

"Tomorrow... for one night."

"Stop her from going."

Joe raised both his hands. "How? Got any ideas?"

Angelo shook his head and rolled his eyes. "Sofia said Nina's the stubborn one in the family. I'll get someone to follow her."

Joe pondered the proposal. "Not the police."

"When the new Tunisian government disbanded the secret police, many of them went into what you call private practice."

Joe stared at him for five seconds. "No. They'll be spotted. I'm always telling her to be careful. If she doesn't see them, Omar's men might."

"At least get her flight numbers."

"She's already mad at me. Call your relative at the airport. Maybe he can find out. Before she leaves she'll call, and if I ask which flight she's taking she'll think I'm planning something. I don't want to make her nervous."

Nina and Monique walked along Via dei Condotti, two blocks from the Spanish Steps.

They stopped in front of a display window at the Gucci store. Nina had wandered the street many times but bought nothing. The fashions and accessories of Prada, Louis Vuitton and Stuart Weitzman, didn't fit into her budget. Monique's wallet produced a constant supply of hundred euro bills. *She's getting more than a sex and bracelets from Omar.*

"Where does Omar work," Nina asked.

"An international shipping company."

Nina nodded. "What does he do?"

"I don't know... must be important, he's paid well."

"Does he ever come to Rome?"

"The job keeps him busy."

They left Gucci, stepped into the crowded street and walked past the Bulgari and Prada stores, stopping at the window of a small boutique.

Nina looked at the prices of the women's clothing on display. *Even the small shops think we should pay extra for their name.*

"Wait until you see the villa. It has big pool and a hot tub."

"Is it nice?"

"I stayed there once, it's beautiful."

"Will he meet us at the airport?"

"No. He'll send a car to get us. The last time I went a new Range Rover picked me up outside baggage claim." Monique headed to the store's door. "Come on, I need a new dress."

Wish she'd talk more about him. I can't keep asking questions.

###

Majid sat at his desk while Omar finish counting a stack of five hundred euro notes. "Fifteen thousand, correct?"

"Yes."

"Tell Jamal to get rid of his galley girl, she's seen enough."

"He did... last week." He grinned. "She was fun while she lasted."

Majid raised his eyebrows. "Be careful. I can't protect you if Jamal catches you playing with one of his personal toys."

"Five trips and five pleasurable late night meetings. I'm still here, he hasn't caught me yet."

Majid shook his head. "You're crazier than I thought."

Omar smiled and raised his eyebrows. "Monique is coming tomorrow, she's bringing a friend. Can they stay at the villa?"

"Sure, call Ayisha. What's her friend's name?"

"Nina, you want to meet her?"

Majid shook his head. "I'm leaving tonight, I'll be in Tehran."

"The next shipment?"

"Yes."

"Can I use your car and driver to pick them up at the airport?"

Majid nodded. "Tell Kojo, he'll set it up for you."

"I guess I must take care of both women," Omar said tapping his chest.

"Be careful. You play more than you work."

"I'm here when you need me."

"Watch what you say to them."

Chapter IX

THE VILLA

The chauffeured Mercedes pulled up to the iron gate in the ten-foot high concrete wall. It swung open, and the car drove to the front entrance of a sprawling two-story villa.

Nina's eyes opened wide as she surveyed the exterior of the house. The large windows reflected the cloudless sky as if they were mirrors. Except for creamy beige accents around the windows and doors, the white stucco walls reminded her of Santorini, Greece. *The only thing missing is a deep blue domed roof, centered with a simple cross.*

The driver stopped near five half-circle steps leading to a landing and the entrance. A short middle-aged woman, wearing a hijab, stepped from the house. She walked to the edge of the steps and watched as the chauffeur opened the car door.

"See what I mean?" Monique asked.

Nina examined the massive double wooden doors. "We're staying here?"

"Wait until you look inside," Monique said as she stepped from the car.

Nina slid across the seat and got out.

"Good afternoon, madam," the woman said to Monique.

Monique ignored the greeting. "Her name is Ayisha. She'll take care of everything we need."

Nina smiled and nodded. "Hello Ayisha, nice to meet you. My name is Nina."

The driver opened the trunk and Nina stepped beside him to get her bag.

"Don't worry, he'll bring them inside," Monique said. As she walked up the steps and entered the house, she turned to Ayisha. "Hold the door for Nina!"

Nina frowned on her way up the steps. *That wasn't nice.* "I'll follow you, Ayisha." When she passed through the doorway she stopped and gasped at the surrounding beauty.

Monique waited for her in a foyer with a marble floor and white walls accented in the color gold. At the end of the hall stood a three-tier gilded fountain on blue tile.

Monique led her to a corridor off the foyer. "I'll stay in the same bedroom I used last time," she said.

"Please follow me madam," Ayisha said, turning to Nina "I'll show you to your bedroom. I'm sure you'll be comfortable."

"You don't need to call me madam. Nina is fine."

"Thank you, this way." She reached a door and stepped into a bedroom.

As Nina crossed the threshold, she hesitated. A canopied bed with a carved wooden headboard, and two night tables accented in reddish gold caught her eye. Through the door to the bath, black tiles surrounded a large marble tub. "This place is beautiful. Who lives here?"

Ayisha stared at her for a moment. "No one. The villa is used to entertain guests."

"Omar's friends?"

She smiled. "No. Majid Ziyad, Omar's employer owns the house. Business associates and important customers meet here." Ayisha slipped out the door.

Nina sat on the bed and surveyed the room. "Someone named Majid has a lot of money." She furrowed her brow. *Joe didn't mention his name. Wonder who he is?* There was a tap on the door. She opened it, looked down and pulled her overnight bag into the room.

As she dropped the bag on the bed and unzipped it, Monique walked in wearing a tiny white bikini. "You like it?"

Nina smiled and raised her eyebrows. "Doesn't hide much, but it looks great on you."

"No, I mean the villa."

Both women laughed.

"Oh, yes, it's beautiful,"

"Wait until you see the rest of the house." Monique headed to the door. "I'll be at the pool, it's at the back, past the portico. Put on your bathing suit and join me."

A dip in the pool sounds great. I need to keep her talking. Nina dug out her emerald bikini, changed into it, and removed a sheer wrap from her bag. In the bathroom, she turned in a circle in front of the mirror. *This one is small enough. How does she dare walk around in that tiny thing?* She shrugged at the mirror and left the room.

Not knowing which way to go, she returned to the foyer, turned and passed between a living and dining room. *Gaudy. Way too much white and gold.*

When she came to an open area where marble columns supported a stucco ceiling painted with intricate flowers and vines, she stopped. *She's right. It's a portico, not a patio.*

She spotted Monique waving to her from an umbrella covered table near the pool. Out of the corner of her eye, she noticed Ayisha watching from a doorway. As she reached the table and pulled out a chair, Ayisha stepped beside her.

"Would you like something to eat and drink... wine?" the housekeeper asked.

Nina nodded, "Red, please?"

"Red for both of us," Monique ordered.

"Yes, madam." She scurried away.

"Why don't you like her?" Nina asked.

"Ayisha? She's all right, but she's only a servant."

Surprised at her friend's callousness, Nina changed the subject. "I thought Omar would be here."

Monique stood. "He'll come soon. Let's sit by the pool."

They sat at the edge and dangled their feet in the water.

"Ayisha said a man named Majid owns this house. Omar's lucky to have such good friends," Nina said.

Monique pursed her lips. "I've never met him." She raised a finger to her mouth. "It's best if you don't mention his name."

"Why?"

"I'll tell you later, just don't. Omar will be angry. He's doesn't want people to know about his private life."

"Why?"

"He doesn't want the authorities to know how much money he makes."

Omar arrived at eight and went into the house to change into a bathing suit. He returned to the poolside table where Ayisha cleared away half-full plates of food. She had placed a bottle of scotch beside the bottle of wine in front of the two women.

"When did you and Monique meet?" Omar asked.

"Two months ago, at work." She didn't take her eyes off him. *Good looking. His dark hair and complexion make his green eyes glow against his olive skin.*

Monique interrupted. "Nina found a wonderful apartment and needed a roommate."

When she didn't continue speaking, Nina did. "How long have you and Monique been together?"

"A little over six months. We met in Egypt."

Omar lifted the wine bottle and half-filled their glasses. He poured himself scotch.

Monique held out her glass. "Fill it to the top."

Aware Omar was staring at her, Nina covered her glass with her hand. "No thank you."

"Do you enjoy being a flight attendant?" he asked.

"Yes, I love to travel. What type of work do you do?"

"International shipping... at the port."

Monique downed half the wine in her glass. She held it to Omar, and he refilled it.

"Sounds interesting," Nina said. "I'll bet owning a company keeps you busy."

"It does, but it's not my company. I work for MZ Shipping and Export. One day I'll start a business."

"That will be nice... lots of travel."

"Yes."

Monique emptied what remained in the wine bottle into her glass. "Enough talk about work." She turned to Omar. "You should come to visit Rome and stay with us."

"The next month will be busy. One day I'll plan a trip."

Ayisha walked to the table and replaced the empty wine bottle with a full one.

Nina waited until she stepped away and smiled at Omar. "When you come we'll show you Rome." She stood. "Excuse me, I'll be back in a minute." She walked away from the pool.

Tall... and beautiful, Omar thought as Nina walked into the house. He smiled at Monique. "I'm glad you found a good friend when you moved to Rome."

Unsteady in her chair, she sipped more wine. "Me too."

He took her hand, lifted the bottle of wine and led her to the nearby hot tub. She held his arm and leaned against his side as he helped her into the water and refilled her glass.

"You look wonderful but you don't need this." He unhooked her top, slid the bottom from her legs and pulled her to him pressing her back against his chest.

She leaned her head against his shoulder and slurred her words. "We shouldn't do it here, Nina will be back soon."

Omar kissed her neck. "Good, the tub is big enough for the three of us."

###

Nina, now wearing a floral sun dress, strolled to the tub and looked at them. She bit the inside of her cheek trying not to show her surprise. *Should have taken longer to change.*

"Are we embarrassing you?" Omar asked.

"Of course not." She stepped to the table and took a seat.

"Join us," he said. "The water feels good. Leave your dress on the chair."

Here we go. I know your culture. Don't raise your hopes. "Love to, but tonight, I can't."

"Why?" Monique asked.

"It's the wrong time of the month."

Omar's eyes widened. "Best if you don't. Another time."

She picked up her glass of wine and pushed away from the table. "I'm tired. You have fun. We'll talk in the morning."

"I'm leaving early," Omar said. "See you next time you visit."

"Yes, next time, or in Rome when you come. Good night."

###

Glad to be alone in her room and away from the awkward scene at the pool, Nina folded her dress and laid it on the bed. She removed the robe from a hook on the bathroom door and slipped into it when there was a soft knock on the door. "Who is it?"

"Ayisha."

She opened the door. "Please, come in."

Nina studied the woman. A white work tunic over black pants hid her small frame. A colorful hijab covered her hair. Nina focused on thin lines etched into Ayisha's tanned face. *Hard to tell her age. Fifty?*

"Is something wrong, madam?"

"No, Ayisha. I'm tired."

"Please do not take offense. Why are you here?"

Surprised at the woman's question, Nina stared at her. "I don't understand."

"I've watched you since you arrived. You are courteous, and like a lady, you are careful what you say and do. You're not like the people who come here."

"What do you mean, Ayisha? I'm no different from others."

"You don't act like the women who are brought here. Most have no honor and, sometimes bad things happen."

"What bad things? Monique and I aren't in danger, are we?"

"No, but you must be careful."

Nina paused and stared at her. "What about you?"

"I'm fine. When I meet good people, it makes me realize my grandchildren will one day live a good life."

"Where do they live?"

"Here in Tunis, with me. I'm from Iraq. My daughter and her husband are dead. Most of my family died in the war."

Nina shook her head. "I'm sorry."

"One day we will leave here."

"Where will you go?"

Ayisha smiled. "I've saved most of the money I'm paid. We'll go to Europe and get away from people in the business of destroying lives."

"I don't understand."

Ayisha looked over her shoulder, turned, and closed the door.

"I can tell you are different. You care how you treat people. Be careful. It's best if you don't come here again. Omar is not a person you want as your friend."

Nina took a deep breath. "What's wrong? Tell me, I won't say anything to Monique."

Ayisha lowered her voice to a whisper. "Listen to what I say. I'm here because I need this job."

Chapter X

WORRIED MEN

Joe, Angelo, Sergio and DEA Agent Paul Sacca sat at the table in Colonel Aldo's conference room.

Paul looked at Joe. "Did Duffy say anything to you about the last meeting?"

"Yeah."

"He told me the FBI wanted to be part of the investigation."

Out of the corner of his eye, Joe watched Angelo leaf through papers in front of him. *Guess I'm stuck with this one.* He nodded. "They do, but I don't know what happened. I'll ask the boss."

Colonel Aldo entered and the four men stood. Everyone waited until he took a seat.

"You have news for us, Angelo?" Aldo asked.

Joe raised a finger. "Sir, before we start, did you receive an inquiry from the FBI?"

Aldo smiled and stared at him for a moment. "Yes, from our friend Agent Robert Duffy. I sent a note to the embassy telling them I forwarded it to the Chief of Staff. He's a busy man, but I'm sure when he reads it, he'll approve. For now the Carabinieri, the Marshals Service, and your DEA will do the best job they can."

Approval may take a month, Joe thought. When the colonel wanted something done, he did it and told his boss later. This time he wanted the request to go up the slow to react chain of command. *I love this guy.*

"Please start, Angelo," Aldo said.

He removed a notebook from his pocket. "Miami is meeting with Omar."

Joe realized what Angelo was doing. *Doesn't want to say it's in Tunis. Good job, Ang.*

Paul turned to him and frowned. "Isn't he going out with Omar's girlfriend?"

Angelo shrugged.

"Is Miami involved in drugs?" Aldo asked.

"No, sir," Angelo replied. "Joe and I did a complete background check. Nothing on file. Never stopped or questioned by the police."

Aldo squinted and focused on the tabletop for five seconds. "Tell me about this person you call Miami."

Joe leaned forward. *Quick, what do we tell him? I need to change the subject.* Before he opened his mouth, Angelo continued and the tightness in his chest disappeared.

"Italian citizen, a patriot, good job, anti-drug, comes from a good family. Horrified when the five agents were killed."

"Are they meeting outside Italy?" Paul asked.

Angelo nodded.

Paul stared at him for a moment. "Where?"

"Didn't tell us."

"When is he coming back?" Paul asked.

Joe couldn't keep quiet any longer. Paul was fishing for information. "In a day or two."

"Traveling by plane?"

I'm not that damn stupid. The answer to the question may lead to Nina's identity. "Didn't say where the meeting was being held. We weren't told how they are getting there, or how long it would last." Joe shrugged. "Could have traveled by car, ferry, or plane."

"Miami isn't telling you much," Paul said.

Angelo leaned forward. "True. Not yet, but trust must be shown by both sides."

Sergio shifted in his chair. "Let us talk to him."

Angelo's body stiffened. "It's not going to happen."

Aldo held up a hand. "Agent Sacca and Lieutenant Lacona, your superiors may not like it, but I've made my decision. I won't place someone's life in danger. Trust Angelo and Joe and respect their request. Our first priority is to find the person leaking information. After that, we'll get Omar so you both can solve your case."

Paul raised his eyebrows and nodded. "I understand, sir. DEA told me to ask. I'll tell them to stay calm."

"Good. Anything else for me?"

"No, sir," Angelo said. "We need to discuss a few things with Paul and Sergio."

Aldo stood. When no one else spoke, he glanced at Angelo. "Call us after you debrief Miami." He left the room.

Joe and Angelo cornered the two narcotics investigators.

"Listen," Joe said. "No one is trying to cut you guys out of the investigation. The informant told us we had to keep his identity secret. I promise you'll get everything we find out. Angelo and I would appreciate you not trying to corner us in front of Colonel Aldo."

"You're speaking for both of you?"

Joe ground his teeth, his pulse raced. *I'll whip your ass if you...*

Angelo stepped in front of Sergio. "Lieutenant Lacona. When I speak, or Inspector Costa speaks, we speak for each other. I suggest you remember that if you wish for you career as a Carabinieri officer to flourish."

Sergio took a breath. "Sorry, sir."

Paul interceded. "Both of us are being pressured. We'll handle it."

"It's best if we don't defy Colonel Aldo," Sergio said.

Yeah, if you want to keep your job.

After the meeting Joe walked with Angelo to his office. He pulled a chair, in front of Angelo's desk and took a seat. "Don't be angry at him."

"I'm not. He's doing what the academy taught him."

"What do you mean?"

"When you're an officer of the Carabinieri, you can throw your weight around," Angelo said as he grinned and tapped the captain's insignia on his uniform. "He made the mistake of doing it in front of someone whose ass is a little heavier." He removed his note pad from his pocket and placed it in the center desk drawer. "I wish we didn't have to lie to them."

"Don't worry. Their superiors feel left out when they aren't told everything that's happening. We've got to stick to our plan."

Angelo nodded. "Did you hear from Nina?"

"I told her not to call." Joe stared at him. "You didn't do anything crazy, did you?"

"No. They may watch to see if someone follows them."

"Nina's smart. She won't place herself in danger. Doesn't make me worry any less, but I can't do anything about it now."

"You're right," Angelo said. "I can't wait to pick her brain. She'll come back loaded with information. Come to dinner at my house tonight. I'll call Sofia."

"I'd love to but she'll ask why Nina isn't with me."

"Yeah. Then we must come up with more lies. We'll meet again in the morning."

Chapter XI

THE INFORMANTS

Majid got up from his desk and walked to the couch. He took his cell phone from his pocket and tapped the screen.

A deep voice with a Polish accent came over the speaker. "Are you are well today, sir?"

"Yes Gustav. Have you been to Krakow to visit your mother?"

"No. I called her this morning. She's better."

"From the sound of your message you've been busy."

"Yes, the captain is stupid."

"Tell me everything he wrote."

"Miami will talk to Omar."

"Anything else?"

"Yes. The name 'Paul', the letters 'DEA' and the words 'wants in', at the bottom of the page."

"Nothing more?"

"No, sir."

"Good work, Gustav. Miami must be a code for the person. Try to find out his real name. Check your mail in a few days. I'm sending an extra payment."

"Thank you, sir."

After Nina's safe return, Joe waited for her at a table in the Target restaurant on the corner of Via Modena and Via Torino, a block west of Piazza della Repubblica. That afternoon she called, and he asked her to meet him at nine for dinner.

During the week people filled the sidewalk tables and the street level dining room. Few used the one hundred-seat room down a narrow flight of stairs. He had arranged for a corner table so they would be away from other customers. An open bottle of wine and two glasses stood on the white table cloth in front of him.

Nina stepped from the stairway and headed in his direction. He stood and smiled. She wore red heels, a short skirt with a red lace blouse, and carried a large handbag over her shoulder. *Wow! Stunning. Loves red and always dresses to the nines.* What he needed at the moment was to hold her. He pulled her into his arms and they kissed. "Thank God you're back. No more trips to Tunisia, please."

"You worry too much. Everything went well, and I learned quite a bit."

He took her hand. "Glad you did but don't press your luck. I love you and don't want anything to happen. Let's have wine."

Joe sat with his back against the wall and Nina sat to his right.

She looked around the near empty dining room. "Why do you always pick a table against the wall?"

"Habit."

"Is anyone joining us?"

He slipped his hand to her knee, squeezed and watched her jump. "I told Angelo we wanted to be alone."

"Good."

"Can you go with me to his office tomorrow morning?"

"Sure, what time?"

"I'll pick you up at ten."

"There are a thousand things to tell you about the trip. I made notes."

"Besides what you told me on the phone, is anything urgent? Something we need to talk about right now?"

"Not really."

Joe smiled and took her hand. "Good. Let's enjoy the evening."

She leaned towards him, her eyes sparkling with excitement. "If I stay at your apartment you won't need to pick me up in the morning." Her hand slid to his upper thigh, and she kissed him as she lifted her handbag. "I brought everything I need."

"Beautiful Italian women are so romantic." He tickled her side and winked.

"Yes and jealous." She grabbed his chin and pulled him close to her. "For your own safety, concentrate on this Italian woman."

"I plan to, all night long."

At ten-thirty, the next morning, Joe, Nina and Angelo sat near the coffee table in Angelo's office.

Angelo read two pages of notes Nina provided him and smiled. "You did a good job listening."

"And I kept good notes."

"Angelo and I will go over them and write a report before we speak to the others. Will Monique help us?"

Nina shook her head and sighed. "No, she loves him."

Joe squinted and paused. "Is there anything we can do to turn her against him?"

"No. From what I saw, she'll do anything for him."

"That's the answer," Angelo said.

"What do you mean?" Nina asked.

It didn't take Joe long to figure out Angelo's line of thinking. He grinned and turned to Nina. "We'll use that to our advantage. If he's in danger, will she still want help him?"

"Yes. Like I said, she'd do anything."

"Good," Joe said. "If we can convince her the only way to keep him alive is to help us... she'll agree."

Nina tilted her head to the side and glanced at both men. "Maybe, but he helped kill the agents on the boat, how can he escape that?"

"He won't," Angelo said. "His fate is sealed. She's the only one who may benefit."

"I don't understand. She'll lose the man she loves."

"And she'll remain alive," Joe said. "She knows too much. The people in Majid's organization won't let her live."

Mia knocked on the doorframe and brought in a tray with three cups of espresso.

"Thank you, Mia." Nina said, as her cousin left the room.

"Did Omar say anything about Majid or his job?" Joe asked.

"No. Monique told me not to mention Majid's name in front of him. He only said he worked for him and was busy. Monique was the only thing on his mind."

"What about this lady, Ayisha?" Angelo asked.

"She's nice... we talked. She doesn't like Omar or his boss."

Joe raised a finger. "You said she might leave if given the opportunity?"

"Yes. She wants to come to Europe. Everyone in her family in Iraq is dead, except her two grandchildren." She looked at her watch. "Anything else? I have a flight to Milan and back, later today."

"Tonight?" Joe asked.

"If you pick me up at the airport."

Joe stood and took her into his arms. "I'll be there."

Chapter XII

WHO IS MIAMI

Majid leaned back in the chair and glanced around the office. Gustav seldom provided him with inaccurate information. He couldn't get their last conversation out of his mind. It worried him that Italian authorities had Omar's name and may try to use him as an informant. The problem was he had no proof, and nothing had hindered their operations. *This is not a court, I need no proof.*

Omar entered and lowered himself into a chair in front of the desk. "You wanted me?"

Majid hesitated before he spoke. "There's a problem and your name is on it."

"I've done nothing wrong."

"Someone in Italy said a police informant talked to you."

Blood drained from Omar's face as he jumped from the chair. "That's crazy. Whoever told you that is lying."

Majid locked his eyes on him. *One wrong word and you are dead.* "Sit."

Omar dropped to the edge of the chair. "When did I ever talked to anyone I haven't known for a long time?"

"Are you friends with a man named Paul?"

"An American name. No."

"What about someone called Miami?"

"Like the city? No." His eyes settled on the floor for three seconds before he raised his head. "Where did you get this information?"

"It doesn't matter. If anyone approaches you, tell me. Don't play games. Understand?"

"Of course."

Exhausted by the end of the day, Angelo sat at his desk daydreaming. Nina did a fabulous job, but he and Joe agreed she wouldn't get near Tunis or Omar again.

Mia poked her head into his office. "A man is here to clean. I told him you were busy."

"Send him in, I'm leaving." He scooped up the papers on his desk and dropped them into the two-drawer safe, spinning the combination lock as the man entered.

"Good evening, Captain."

"Hello Gustav, how are you?"

"Fine, sir."

"How is your mother? Doing better I hope."

"Much better, thank you."

"Tell her I said hello." He picked up his hat and headed to the door.

That same evening, Monique sat up in the hotel room bed, and watched television. The cell phone on the nightstand rang, and she turned on the speaker. "Hello."

"Where are you?" Omar asked.

Sounds mad. Something's wrong. "In London. Is everything all right?"

"I hope so. Are you friends with a man named Paul?"

"No."

"What about someone called Miami?"

"No. What are you talking about?"

"Nothing important. Majid wasn't friendly today. I don't know if he trusts me. He said someone in Italy mentioned my name." His tone softened. "How's my lover tonight?"

"Fine, I miss you. I thought you were mad."

"No. Did you enjoy yourself at the villa?"

"Yes, I love it there."

He hesitated. "We must do it again... maybe next month."

"I can't wait that long."

"Okay, sooner. The next two weeks will be busy. Call when you get back to Rome."

"I will. I love you."

"Me too... talk to you later."

She set the phone on the nightstand. *He didn't say he loved me.*

Nina lay on the couch in Joe's apartment and moaned as he rubbed her feet. The phone startled her when it rang. As she snatched it from the coffee table, she looked at the caller ID. *Monique.* She turned to Joe and raised a finger to her lips. "Hi

Monique... Yes, give me a second." She lowered her feet to the floor and motioned for him to get a pen and paper.

He leapt to a small desk and returned with a notepad and pencil.

"Okay. Who did you say?" she asked.

After a momentary pause, she cocked her head to the side and scribbled 'Paul' and 'Miami' on the paper. "Never heard of them... why?" After listening for thirty seconds, she spoke. "Okay, tomorrow afternoon." She ended the call.

Joe glanced at the paper and froze. "What was that about... why did you write those names?"

Nina flinched and glared at him. "Monique asked if they were my friends. Why are you upset?" She paused, not taking her eyes from his. "Omar called her and asked if she knew them. He seemed to be worried. She told him she didn't and asked me if I did."

He took a deep breath and sat beside her. "In a way, you don't know them. Or I should say don't know of them."

"Do you?"

"Yes."

"How? That's impossible... you've never met Monique and haven't talked to Omar. Who the hell has the name Miami?"

Joe glanced at the blank flat screen television and shook his head. He took her hand in both of his and looked into her eyes. "You."

Her mouth dropped opened. "Me?"

"It's a long story. Angelo and I gave you that name."

Her eyes widened as she pulled her hand away. "Isn't Nina good enough? Are you both turning me into a joke?"

She slid her hand to her back as he tried to take it.

"Don't be mad. Please let me explain."

She glared at him as she leaned away and crossed both arms over her chest.

"After you told Angelo and me what you found in Monique's room, we notified Colonel Aldo and the American and Italian narcotics investigators. I told Angelo I didn't want your name in the report. I love you and don't want you getting hurt. We made up a story about a confidential informant who wouldn't talk to us if we mentioned their name. We gave you the name Miami."

Nina did not move her eyes from him for a full five seconds. "Why did you tell Aldo and the others?"

"You're now a big part of the investigation. Ang and I didn't want the others to do something stupid and send everyone into hiding. Police often give an informant a code name to protect their identity."

She pressed her lips together. "Couldn't you pick something nicer than a city name?" Nina saw him try to hide a smile. *If he laughs I'll punch him.*

"Men don't think of those things. I wanted to pick Goddess, but everyone would realize it was you."

"You're not getting away that easy. Who is Paul?"

"A DEA agent at the embassy."

She scooted next to him. "Joe... do I need to be concerned for my safety?"

"I don't think so, but remember I said this may be dangerous. I'm calling Angelo." He slid the phone from his pocket and made the call.

"I want to listen."

He tapped the screen, and they listened to the loud ring.

"Hello," Angelo said.

"You sleeping?"

"I was."

"You better get up, we need to talk. I'm with Nina and you're on the speaker."

Angelo moaned. "Okay, I'm awake. What the hell is so important?"

"Monique called Nina from London and asked her if she ever heard the name Paul or Miami."

Five silent seconds passed.

"Are you there, Angelo?"

"Yes. Did you say Nina's with you?"

"Yes," Nina said. "We're at Joe's apartment."

"Stay with Joe for a couple of days."

She shook her head. "I can't. Monique will wonder what happened and she may say something to Omar."

"Damn it," Joe said. "I'll be in your office at nine. We need to figure out what happened. Nina and I will talk about her safety tonight. See you in the morning."

Nina walked to the kitchen and returned with two glasses of wine. "How bad is it?"

"Bad. Someone is giving Majid's organization information, but you're safe."

"How can you say that?"

"Angelo and I are the only two people on earth who know you are Miami. Your notes are in my safe and the reports we wrote don't mention your name... they only refer to a person codenamed Miami."

"Then how did Omar get the names?"

Joe rubbed his chin and looked around the room. "The only people given those names are the small group that met with the colonel. The person passing information to Majid and Omar must be close to one of us."

"What should I do?"

"Nothing. Act normal around Monique and don't ask too many questions."

"At the end of the call she didn't sound concerned. I'll only see her for a short time before my flight tomorrow."

"Good. You'll be able to tell if something's wrong. Call me immediately if you think there's a problem."

Chapter XIII

IT'S ME

The next morning, Joe wasted no time. He woke Nina early, kissed her and told her to be cautious and not let Monique talk her into anything when she went back to her apartment.

He arrived outside the conference room at the same time as the colonel and hesitated before opening the door. "Good morning, sir."

Aldo nodded. "Good morning. It seems Captain Randi likes to arrange meetings with little notice."

Joe pulled open the door. "Yes, sir. This one is important."

"We'll see."

Aldo entered the room and Joe followed.

Angelo and Paul stood.

The colonel told everyone to take a seat and sat in a chair at the head of the table. He looked at Angelo. "I trust you called us because there's good news."

Angelo tightened his jaw and raised his eyebrows. "No, sir. Most is alarming."

"I've been doing this job for quite a few weeks, not much frightens me anymore, Angelo," Aldo said with a smile. "Tell us why we're here."

Joe sighed when Angelo spoke without notes or a written report. *Documents are never easy to control, even when the people in the room can be trusted.*

Angelo took a breath. "If everyone here had the true name of our informant, he'd be dead. Our leak goes directly to the Ziyad organization."

Aldo stared at him and frowned. "Are you sure?"

"Sir, the informant has not been working for us long. Last night, Joe received information that Majid asked about two names."

Heads turned and everyone looked at each other.

"What names," Aldo asked.

"Paul, and the code name, Miami. The leak is connected to one of us... including Sergio."

Aldo looked at the three men. "Where is Lieutenant Lacona?"

"In Sicily meeting with a Chief Magistrate in Palermo... he'll be back tonight," Paul said.

The colonel raised his elbows to the table, clasped his hands together, and glanced at Angelo. "The accusation you're making is serious."

Angelo's eyes widened. "Yes, sir, but I'm not blaming anyone here."

Joe leaned on the table. "Sir, may I say something?"

"Please do. Hopefully you can shed light on what Angelo said."

"We're not making accusations. But, the informant is someone we know... someone who works in this building."

Aldo pressed his hands against his lips and stared at the table. "Why this headquarters?"

"The Ziyad organization found out about the trawler operation," Angelo said. "They also knew about Saladino's pending arrest. Now they have these names, and the one place both names were mentioned was in this room."

Aldo tapped his fingernails on the table as he looked at Joe and Paul. "Don't take this personally." He turned to Angelo. "What about the U.S. Embassy?"

Joe froze in his chair. He glanced at Paul and to Aldo. "Sir, I'll answer for myself and Paul can follow. There are files in my office about the trawler case and Saladino's arrest. I also have our informant's notes. Everything is locked in my safe and I'm the only one with the combination. In the ambassador's private safe is a lockbox with an embossed lead band around it. Double-sealed envelopes containing every safe combination in the embassy are in the box." He paused and took a deep breath. "The ambassador and the Chief of Security must be present to open the box and reseal it. I'll speak with the ambassador later today." He looked at Paul.

"A large DEA file on the trawler case is in my safe. Saladino's file is next to it. Like Joe, I'm the only one with the combination." He raised his eyebrows. "The name Miami is not written on any document in my office."

Aldo looked at Angelo. "And you?"

"Two small files are in my safe along with my reports of Miami's activities. I did not keep a copy of the notes Miami provided to us."

Aldo rubbed his temple with his index finger. "What I've been told is here. I suggest each of you use the same compartment, and for now, stay away from putting anything on paper. No one could gain access to one of our safes, the answer is simpler. Get your communications devices checked... today." He pursed his lips and glanced at each man. "Do what you must, I want answers, soon."

As Aldo left the room, Joe turned to Paul. "Stay, we need to talk." The door closed. "Remember I told you we'd share anything we learned?"

Paul nodded. "Yeah, you find something helpful?"

The three men sat and Angelo removed a folded paper from his pocket. "Under different circumstances I would give a copy of this to the Anti-Narcotics Group and one to you. Because of the present situation, Joe and I want it to go to as few people as possible."

Joe turned and faced Paul. "Careful with this, it can lead to the identity of our informant."

"Will I need help to act on the information?"

"Yes," Joe said. "But not from DEA or the FBI."

"There's a woman who works for Majid by the name of Ayisha... about fifty years old," Angelo said. "She's in a position to overhear details of his drug operations and she doesn't like what she heard."

"Is she involved?"

Joe shook his head. "No. She's a housekeeper in a villa he owns. It's where he entertains suppliers and dealers outside Tunis."

Angelo handed Paul the paper.

Paul spent a moment looking at the two typed sentences. "Her name, the fact she works at Majid's villa... the address and she wants to get her grandchildren to Europe. Is that all I get?"

"I'm not putting anything else on paper," Angelo said. "She's raising her two grandchildren and she'll tell us everything she knows if we can get her to Europe."

Joe raised a finger. "She may have information to put people in prison for a long time."

"You guys are asking me to get her out? What the hell can I do alone? Tunisia isn't the friendliest place on earth."

Joe grinned. "You're friends with Al Provitti. The CIA has no stake in this poker game, but they may help."

Paul pointed at Angelo. "What about your guys?"

He shrugged and raised his eyebrows. "Tunisia and Italy are trading partners with close relations. Our politicians would raise hell if we're involved."

Joe understood Paul's apprehension. Americans may be blamed for snatching an Iraqi citizen from Tunisia. *I can hear the international uproar.* The CIA Station Chief was the key to the plan. "That's why we mentioned Provitti. The Agency more than likely has locals on the payroll that want to make a few dollars."

Paul smiled. "You two think of everything, don't you? What other feats of magic am I supposed to do?"

"After you talk to Al, let us know what he says," Joe said.

Angelo raised a finger. "One more thing. Whatever you do, don't bring her to Italy."

"Where am I supposed to take her? You don't snatch a family out of North Africa and magically deposit them in a country in Europe. You're talking to Paul Sacca, not Harry Houdini."

"Anywhere. France, Germany, but Italy is out of the question," Angelo said.

Joe smiled. "Provitti will come up with a plan. If they can get her on a Navy ship, she can be flown to one of our bases in Europe."

Paul glanced at the ceiling. "You're not making it easy, Angelo. The ambassador will have to be told."

Joe shrugged. "Sounds like Provitti's problem."

Later that evening Angelo prepared to leave his office. He gathered the papers on his desk and shoved them into a folder in the two-drawer safe. After spending hours mulling over what he might do to find out how Majid got his information, he was no closer to an answer. He closed the safe, spun the dial and turned to his desk.

A pen and pencil caught his eye. He grabbed them and opened the center drawer of the desk. When he looked down, he saw his note pad. A pain shot across his chest as he focused on his scribbled note. He read aloud. "Miami will talk to Omar. Paul, DEA, wants in."

Time stopped and his face contorted. *I went crazy trying to figure out where the information came from and what crazy man provided it. I'm in trouble now.* He snatched the handset from the phone and dialed two numbers. "Glad you're still here, I need to talk to you."

Mia hurried to his desk. "What is it?"

"Did you go into my desk?"

Her eyes locked on his. "No! Why?"

"Things are out of place. Who has access to my office?"

She paused, glanced up, and bit her bottom lip. "Me, you, Colonel Aldo, his secretary and the cleaning crew. Those who guard the building at night may come in with the people who clean."

"Good. Thank you. Are you leaving now?"

"Yes."

"I'll see you in the morning."

Mia left the office. He pulled out his cell phone and set it on the desk.

Joe answered on the second ring. "Hi Angelo."

"I discovered the source of our leak."

"Great. Where?"

"My damn office."

"What? Who?"

"Me. Stupid me."

"Christ, Angelo. What the hell are you saying?"

"Can you come to my office, now?"

"I'll be there in half an hour."

"Don't tell anyone. We need to talk."

Angelo didn't leave his desk while he waited for Joe. *Nineteen years and it may end because of one stupid mistake.* The note kept luring his eyes to the center of the drawer.

Joe strode into the office. "What's this crazy story?"

"Not crazy, dumb."

"What the hell happened?"

Angelo stood and pointed to the inside of his drawer. "Look!"

Joe circled the desk and looked at the open page of the notebook. "Okay. The note you used at the meeting, what's the problem?"

"Read it... out loud."

"Miami will talk to Omar. And at the bottom, Paul, DEA, wants in." Joe's mouth dropped opened, and he looked at Angelo. "Jesus. Both of the names Omar mentioned to Monique." He looked back at the note. "That doesn't tell me how he got them."

Angelo took a breath. "After we got back from the meeting I put my notepad in the desk."

"And didn't lock it?" Joe asked.

He lowered his head and nodded.

"You tell Aldo yet?"

"Hell no. I want to catch this bastard. The colonel and I talked about having cameras installed in different places around the building. I didn't get around to it, but one will be in here before I leave tonight."

Joe focused on the desk. *Work this to our advantage.* Someone with access to the office went through the desk and passed information to Majid. *That's it.* He raised his head and clicked his fingers. "I've got an idea. Why not write another note? We can tell Majid what we want him to hear. It's our chance to get Omar."

"Omar and his girlfriend."

Joe shook his head. "Just Omar... we may need her."

"What the hell should I write?"

"We need to turn them against each other. Monique told Nina Omar's worried about Majid's questions. Let's get a coffee. We'll figure out a way to increase the pressure on both of them."

Chapter XIV

TRUST

The front door opened and Monique walked into the apartment.

"How was London?" Nina asked.

Monique turned a disgusted look to her. "I hate it. People are too serious. They never smile."

"They live too far from the Mediterranean... not enough sun. Is everything okay with Omar?"

"What do you mean?"

"Those names. Is he mad at you?"

"No. Maybe worried I'm seeing someone else. He's jealous."

"That's crazy. He knows you love him, doesn't he?"

"Yes. I'll call him. Everything is fine."

Nina watched her walk to her bedroom. *She's not upset or worried.*

Omar sat in front of Majid's desk. The longer his boss stared at him the more uncomfortable he became.

"Has anyone approached you?"

"No."

"Has anyone mentioned the names Paul or Miami?" Majid asked without moving his eyes from him.

"No, and like I said, I've never heard of them." He didn't like Majid's tone. *Doesn't trust me.* After hours spent trying to figure out who set him up, he was no closer to an answer.

"For your sake, I hope you haven't."

Omar's stomach churned. Images of what may happen to him flashed through his mind. *I need to be careful.* He thought about again asking Majid who told him, but remained silent.

"The next shipment is almost ready," Majid said. "Heroin is only one part of it. The other half is guns and explosives. Offload the drugs near Sicily. Everything else goes to Latakia, Syria."

"Why weapons for the Syrians?"

"The heroin comes through Iran. Bashar al-Assad is their friend... he needs help to fight those trying to overthrow him."

"The *Iran Iris*?"

Majid nodded. "Jamal is ready, see him tomorrow and make arrangements."

Omar stood and his phone rang as he left the office.

###

Monique ran into the living room, her face contorted in terror. "I talked to Omar."

"What happened?" Nina asked.

"He said Majid doesn't trust him. He's suspicious and asked again about the two names. It worries him because someone told Majid he met with an Italian."

Nina shook her head and took Monique's hand. "It's about drugs, isn't it?"

Monique froze and pulled her hand from Nina's. "How do you know?"

"I not stupid. Ever since the police officers were killed the newspapers are full of stories about drugs coming out of Tunis. Why don't you and Omar get away from these drug dealers? All they do is destroy people's lives."

"Omar works at the port and he may see things, but he's not involved. Anyway, only immigrants use drugs."

"What about Italian kids who get addicted to heroin?"

"They're dumb. It's their problem. Omar will soon have enough money saved. He'll leave his wife and we'll be together."

Nina raised her head. "He's married?"

"Yes, but he hates her."

"Do you realize what you're doing?"

"I love him!"

"If he's helping drug dealers and gets caught, the police will come after you."

"They're not smart enough!"

"Don't get angry. I'm concerned. You're my friend."

Monique hugged her. "Sorry."

Nina kissed her on the cheek. "I'm helping my cousin tonight. We'll be late... I'll stay at her house. Don't do anything stupid. Call me if you want to talk."

Chapter XV

THE SET UP

Joe made it back to his apartment by ten thirty and crept in the door. He spotted Nina holding a bathrobe and wearing panties and a bra at the entrance to the hallway.

"Where you been all night?"

He held her face with both hands and smiled "With Angelo. He's about to catch the informant."

"Who is it?" She put on the bathrobe.

"Soon we'll have a name. Why don't you stay tonight?"

"I plan to."

Joe led her across the living room and they dropped onto the couch. "Everything is changing fast. I want you close where I can take care of you."

"Monique's home. She talked to Omar again... he's worried."

"He should be. If they think he's talking to someone, they'll kill him."

"She doesn't realize what she's doing."

Joe shook his head. "Believe me, she knows. It's all about dollar signs."

"Maybe so, but shouldn't we show compassion?"

"My compassion is for the mothers and children of the dead agents." He grabbed her and wrapped his arms around her waist. "My passion is for you."

Nina winked. "I'm taking time off from work."

"Why?"

"Because Monique did."

He cocked his head. "Not planning anything, are you?"

"No."

"Good. Let's relax. Have a glass of wine."

She grabbed his knee, and he squirmed when she squeezed. "Time for more passion... I won't be leaving town for a few days." She pulled him toward the bedroom.

The next morning, DEA Agent Paul Sacca stepped into Joe's office. "Got good news."

"Glad someone does."

Paul dropped into a chair. "Provitti came to see me earlier about the *Iran Iris*."

Joe raised his eyebrows and leaned over his desk. "What about it?"

"Troops in Afghanistan picked up a major Taliban drug trafficker a month ago. They turned him over to the Agency."

"Is he talking?"

"Provitti said he puked all over the table."

Joe smiled. "Anything good come out?"

"The freighter is docked at Bizarte, north of Tunis... captain's name is Jamal Jalili." He handed Joe an aerial photo of the *Iran Iris* at sea.

Joe examined the picture. "Is there more?"

"Yeah. The ship will pick up guns in Croatia."

"What port?"

"An informant works on the docks in Tunis, he trying to find out."

"What do the guns have to do with Omar and the drug case?"

"The *Iran Iris* has a long-term contract to move goods for Majid's company, MZ Shipping and Export. The only reason to make a stop in Tunisia is to pick up Majid's cargo and part of it may be drugs."

"And part of it might not," Joe said.

Paul grinned. "The puker said a large shipment of heroin left Afghanistan a week before his capture. Provitti thinks it moved through Iran and is now in Tunisia."

Joe bit his lip and stared across the room. *Got to feed him something* "We picked up information Omar is in trouble with his boss... no details yet. Who's working the gun case?"

"It's a joint European effort. The Carabinieri are involved. We'll keep an eye on the ship for them."

"We?"

"American assets, surveillance aircraft and an eye in the sky. Sergio is trying to merge the two cases. He wants to take down the drug operation at the same time they get the guns. Keep me informed about Omar." He left the office.

Joe dialed Angelo's number. "You busy? Okay, I'm on my way."

After Joe arrived in Angelo's office and told him everything Paul said, he wondered why Angelo had a smile on his face and seemed disinterested.

Angelo got up from his desk and walked to the coat rack near the door. He tapped the rack. "Come here and tell me if you can see the camera."

After examining the wood and the brass hooks, he shook his head. *What camera?* "No."

Angelo pointed to a hook facing the center of the office. "In this area."

Joe leaned over and focused on a small hole under the hook. "If there's one here, it's in this hole."

"It is."

"Damn, every year these things get smaller." They sat in chairs in front of the coffee table. "Did you get any video yet?"

"The cleaning girl came in before I arrived today... didn't open any drawers."

Joe nodded. "What did you write on the note?"

"From Miami. Omar wants out, needs money fast, help him."

"That'll rattle a few cages."

Angelo leaned back in his chair. "Did Monique tell Nina anything else?"

"No." He glanced at his watch and stood. "I'm going to be late for a meeting at the embassy. I'll see you at eight tonight, I'll tell Nina to be prepared. If what you wrote gets to Majid, things will not go well for Omar."

That evening, Joe, Nina and Angelo sat a table against a wall in a café near Angelo's office. The waiter removed their empty plates and refilled their wine glasses.

Nina stared at both men as she took a drink. She raised her eyebrows. "Everything is happening so fast. You think he'll call her?"

"I'll bet on it," Joe said.

"We need to know the moment he does," Angelo said. "The three officers outside your apartment won't get close but I need to keep them informed. This is serious. Majid will have to go after Omar. Let's hope he forgets about Monique."

"Both of you sound like my father. I'm a big girl, I'll be careful."

Joe placed his hand over hers. "Why don't you stay at my apartment tonight? You can keep in touch with her by phone."

"Please. We've already talked about that."

Angelo took a deep breath and let it out. "Pay attention to whatever Monique says."

Nina shook her head. "Will you both relax... order something... grappa."

"I have heartburn thinking about what can happen. Grappa would add to the fire," Joe said.

The next morning, Joe sighed with relief when Nina called and said Monique heard nothing from Omar.

Angelo called him before he arrived at his office and told him to be in the colonel's conference room as soon as possible. He walked into the empty room and sat.

A minute later Paul entered. "Angelo call you?"

Joe nodded.

"He sounded like he has good news... where is he?"

"Downloading a video... he'll be a few minutes."

Colonel Aldo walked in and both men stood. "Where's Angelo?"

"On his way, sir," Joe said the moment Angelo entered.

Aldo frowned. "You look like hell Captain Randi. When did you last sleep?"

"Not last night... caught the bastard." He set his laptop onto the table and turned the screen toward the colonel.

Aldo motioned the others to his end of the table and Angelo started the video.

Gustav trudged into Angelo's office, glanced at the door and stepped behind the desk. He pulled on the locked safe drawer, turned and opened the center drawer of the desk. Gustav removed Angelo's notepad, took a pen and paper from his pocket, and wrote on it. When he finished, he returned the notepad to the drawer, closed it, and cleaned Angelo's desk. The video ended and everyone took a seat.

"Who is he?" Aldo asked.

"His name is Gustav Sokolski... Polish. He's part of the cleaning crew," Angelo said. "It's my fault, sir. If you wish, I'll remove myself from the case."

"Who set up the surveillance camera?" Paul asked.

Angelo took a breath. "I arranged it."

Joe couldn't allow his partner hang for his mistake. He looked at Colonel Aldo. "Sir, Angelo developed the plan, and caught him."

Aldo nodded. "Was he arrested?"

"Not yet," Angelo said. "I spent last night getting his cell phone records. Early this morning I received authority to monitor his calls."

Paul rubbed his chin. "Has he called Majid?"

"No."

Aldo sighed. "Let's make sure he doesn't."

"Sir, may I suggest we wait," Angelo said. He removed three small pieces of paper from his pocket. "I wrote this on the note he copied. It will turn Majid against Omar."

Aldo read the note and looked at Angelo. "You made a big mistake, but solved our problem. You still have questions to answer about how this happened. Everyone in this room will support you."

"Thank you, sir."

Joe knew a ton of weight had been lifted from Angelo's shoulders. *He screwed up, but no one is perfect.*

"May I add something, sir?" Paul asked.

"Yes."

"The U.S. Navy and Italian Coast Guard are watching the *Iran Iris*. It will pick up guns in Zadar Croatia and offload them in Syria. Late last night I received information it will also carry drugs. Their plan is to transfer the drugs to a small vessel somewhere near Sicily. I passed the information to the Carabinieri Anti-Drug Command here in Rome and they are coordinating with the Special Intervention Group's terrorism investigation."

Angelo's cell phone rang, and he stepped out of the room.

"Anything else?" Aldo asked.

Joe and Paul shook their heads.

Aldo looked at the door. "We'll wait to hear what Angelo says."

Angelo walked in with a smile on his face. "He called Majid and told him everything on the note."

Colonel Aldo spent a moment staring at the wall across the room. "We need to decide if we want to pick him up or let him continue sending out lies."

"His mother in Poland is sick," Angelo said. "If something happens to her, he'll leave. Once we pick him up he'll realize how much trouble he's facing. He'll do anything we ask."

"You sure?" Paul asked.

Angelo grinned. "This is Italy, not the United States."

"Arrest him." Aldo said.

"We should wait until he comes to work tonight, sir," Joe said. "If we arrest him at his house someone may call Majid."

"Good idea," Aldo said. "Thank you for the information Agent Sacca. Tell the ambassador I'll call."

Chapter XVI

THE GAME

Majid thought about what his informant in Rome told him. He made a call on his cell phone and waited.

"Hello," Omar said.

"Where are you?"

"At home."

"I need to see you tonight. My office at nine."

"I'll be there."

Majid ended the call and looked at the tall three-hundred pound African seated on the couch. A white scar sliced across the man's cheek. "Tonight, Kojo. When he leaves his house."

"And his family?" Kojo asked.

Majid shook his head. "The wife and children have no information. They can't hurt us."

"I'll call when it's done."

The man's massive frame filled the doorway as he left the room. *Everyone fears him.*

Angelo looked across his desk at two Carabinieri officers in dark uniforms. Both appeared as if they spent all their off-duty hours lifting weights. "U.S. Marshals Service Inspector Costa, from the American embassy, wants to watch. When he arrives, the three of you wait in the room across the hall. Once Gustav walks into my office, give me a minute alone with him, and then come in."

Joe walked into the office, and Angelo stepped beside him.

"Joe, this is Marco and Nicolas, two men from the Special Operations Group." He placed a hand on Joe's shoulder. "This is my Task Force Co-Leader, Inspector Joe Costa."

Both men nodded and extended their hands.

"Go with them, Joe, and come into my office when they do."

The three men left and Angelo moved an uncomfortable straight-backed chair to the front of his desk.

He dropped into his leather chair, folded his hands, and waited. *I'm going to squeeze this guy until he pops.*

A tingle shot down his spine at the sound of footsteps. He looked at the short Polish man standing in the doorway. *The bastard that helped kill five men.*

"Sorry, sir. I didn't realize you were working late."

"That's okay, Gustav." Angelo pointed to the front of the desk. "Come in... sit. How is your mother?"

Gustav took a seat. "She is well."

"Still at home taking care of herself?" Angelo asked.

"Yes. Once a week she goes to the doctor."

Angelo nodded. "Good. I'm glad she's self-sufficient because you're going to be busy."

Gustav's forehead creased. "Busy?"

"Yes, sending messages."

"Messages?"

Angelo kept his eyes on him and nodded. "The ones I want Majid Ziyad to receive."

Marco and Nicolas, followed by Joe, rushed into the office at the instant Gustav stood. The two Carabinieri grabbed his arms, handcuffed his hands behind his back and shoved him into the seat. Both men stood behind him.

Joe sat on the couch.

Gustav's wide eyes locked on Angelo. His lower lip quivered.

Angelo rose and walked behind him. "Turn this way."

Marco and Nicolas grabbed the back of the chair and jerked it around, almost tipping it.

Gustav swung a foot to the side and stopped himself from falling.

Angelo paused, looked into Gustav's eyes and leaned toward him. "Gustav, you made a very big mistake. There is no doubt in my mind you are responsible for the five narcotics agents being killed." He removed a paper from his pocket and waved it in front of Gustav's face. "A judge issued this warrant for your arrest. Tonight you will not sleep in your soft bed, but I am not sending you to a prison in Rome." He paused and glared at him. "I'm going to find the oldest and nastiest jail in Italy. One with an underground cell just for you." He stepped back. "You will be so far underground, the jail officials will need to pump sunshine to you through a pipe."

Gustav tried to stand but Nicolas crammed him back into the chair.

"Your poor mother will find out you're living the life of a rodent," Angelo said. "I wonder if she'll survive."

Beads of sweat rolled into Gustav's bulging eyes. "Sir, please. I needed money to take care of her."

"You must love her very much. You helped kill two American and three Italian agents for her. What will she think when she's told you murdered police officers for money?"

Gustav lowered his head. "I'm sorry. All I did was pass information. No one told me they were going to die."

"It's too late. I'm not sorry for you. Life in an Italian prison may not be all you face. Look at the man seated in front of you. He's an American investigator. He told me his government wants to take you to their court where they have the death penalty." Angelo turned to Joe. "Don't they still use the electric chair in America, Inspector Costa?"

Gustav grimaced and his eyes widened. His legs and hands trembled.

Joe slid to the edge of the couch. "Florida does... two thousand, three-hundred volts. It's old, sometimes sparks come out of it. Takes a long time to die."

Angelo looked at the little man. "Of course Gustav, you'll be able to stay in a nice American prison cell before they fry your brain."

Gustav's breathing became short gulps of air. "My mother needs help."

"And now you need my help. You will do everything I tell you, and tell me everything you know, or I guarantee you will rot in a hole worse than hell."

Angelo stared at his captive and remained silent.

"What do you want from me?" Gustav asked, his voice cracking.

"For you to start talking, but not tonight. Consider my proposal. I want an answer in the morning." He motioned to the door. "Take him to his new home."

Marco and Nicolas yanked him to his feet and shoved him out the door.

Angelo walked behind his desk and sat. He opened the bottom right hand drawer and removed a bottle of Courvoisier and a pair of etched whiskey glasses. "Would you like a small drink?"

Joe smiled. "It's a sin to let fine liquor go to waste."

Angelo half-filled the glasses and handed one to Joe. "Now for our next bit of magic." He raised his glass in front of his American partner and smiled.

XVII

THE HIT

When Omar received Majid's call, the first thing that came to mind were the questions he asked about Paul and Miami. Those two names meant nothing to him. *It must be about the next shipment.* Majid was successful because he was cautious. He seldom discussed business over the phone, and when he did, they spoke with coded words. Guns going to Syria had to be what he wanted to discuss.

Omar walked from his apartment building with a smile on his face. The next trip on the *Iran Iris* would be dangerous but profitable. Majid agreed to pay him double his customary fee because of the weapon's shipment. Drug trafficking worried the Tunisian and Italian governments but guns and explosives were a concern to countless countries, including the United States, members of the European Union, and many neighbors in North Africa. *I'll soon make enough money to set myself up in business.* He wanted to keep Monique in his life, and his family at his side.

He approached his parked Toyota, stopped at the curb and unlocked the door. Before he opened it, bullets shattered the back window and slammed into the trunk. He doubled over in pain, grabbed his side, and dropped to the ground. The crack of rifle fire and the sound of bullets penetrating the car made him roll against the Toyota and press as much of his body as possible against it. Tires screeched and a black sedan sped past his car. Glass shattered and the Toyota's interior erupted in flames.

Majid leaned back on the couch with his eyes closed. He jumped to his feet at a knock on the door.

Kojo walked into the office.

"Is it done?" Majid asked.

"Yes. He died beside his car."

Majid nodded. "Thank you, Kojo. What car did you use?"

"A stolen Mercedes. We set it on fire when we finished."

"Good. Tell Jamal Omar had an accident and will not make the trip."

"The captain may ask for more money."

Majid smiled. "He's done this a long time. Many people disappeared in those years. A demanding person is an unhealthy person."

"You want me to go on the ship?"

Majid seldom went anywhere without Kojo. Tunis was not a dangerous city, but his association with the traffickers in Iran made him cautious. *They is always someone who will do it for less money.*

"No, call Yassine. Tell him to find Omar's girlfriend."

Majid walked to his desk and picked up a folded paper. He handed it to the large African man. "This is her name, address and telephone number."

"What should he do when he finds her?"

"Tell him to call me. I have instructions I want him to follow."

Kojo stared at him. "I can do this for you."

Majid tapped the large man's shoulder. "Yassine is closer. You've always been at my side. I need you with me."

Chapter XVIII

NINA'S PLAN

A scream ripped Nina from a dream. She leapt from the bed and raced to Monique's room. "What happened? What's wrong?"

Monique sat on the edge of the bed sobbing, her hands pressed against her face. She raised her head. "Someone tried to kill Omar. He's hurt."

"Where is he?"

"In Tunis, he thinks it was Majid."

Nina's mouth dropped open. "His boss?"

"Yes. He has to leave Tunisia, but doesn't know where to go. He'll hide and call tomorrow. What should I do? If Majid finds out he's still alive someone will try to kill him again. There must be a safe place to go."

Nina scanned the walls. *Joe and Angelo can't arrest people in the Middle East.* She knelt in front of Monique and took her hands. "Athens is the best place. The city is big and he'll be safe."

Monique hugged her. "Good idea. I'll meet him there."

A sickening feeling invaded Nina's stomach. *No. What is she thinking?* "Meet him! Have you lost your mind? People tried to kill him."

"I love him," Monique sobbed. "I need to help."

Nina stood. "Are you sure he'll call again?"

"Yes, tomorrow."

"Can you call him?"

"No, he won't answer his phone. He's afraid Majid can trace it." She buried her face in the pillow.

"Do nothing. I'll call a friend in Athens and ask if he can help." She ran to her bedroom, closed the door and dialed her phone. When Joe answered, she whispered. "Monique said Majid tried to kill Omar." She listened to him rant for fifteen seconds.

"No, I can't come now and don't come here. In the morning I'll meet you at your office." She pulled the phone from her ear, looked at it and listened to Joe's voice, but not his words. After five seconds, she interrupted. "I'll be at the embassy at eight thirty."

###

Joe didn't sleep after Nina's call and arrived at the embassy thirty minutes early. Nina stood in the lobby, waiting. "Angelo's on his way." He kissed her. "Let's go to my office."

Angelo, carrying a tie, arrived two minutes after they settled into chairs. "What the hell happened?" He looked at Nina sitting behind Joe's desk.

"Let Nina explain," Joe said.

"Did Joe tell you anything?" she said leaning on the desk.

"Yes. Omar told your roommate Majid tried to kill him."

She nodded. "Someone shot him and he needs to leave Tunisia but has to get money first. I suggested Athens because it would be easy to hide in the city. She wants to meet him in Greece."

Angelo grinned. "You suggested Athens?"

"Yes."

"Damn, you... are... good."

She cocked her head. "Remember, I'm the quiet one who listens. Italian police can arrest him in the EU."

Angelo nodded. "We'll ask them pick him up on our European Arrest Warrant."

"Will Greece honor an Italian warrant?" Nina asked.

Angelo nodded. "They can't refuse."

Joe glanced at him. "Any good contacts with their police?"

"We won't have a problem. Is Monique still in the apartment?" he asked Nina.

"Yes, waiting for a call."

"We need to find out where he'll be," Joe said to her. "Please listen. If Majid tried to kill Omar, he may try to kill you and Monique."

"That's crazy! Why?"

"Both of you spent time with Omar just before this happened. Sooner or later he'll wonder if that night at the villa has something to do with the information he's getting."

"I've never seen Majid."

Joe sighed. "It doesn't matter. You're Monique's friend, and you were there."

"Have you noticed my men outside the apartment?" Angelo asked.

Nina looked around the room and lowered her gaze to the desktop. "I didn't realize it would get this bad." She brushed lint off of her sleeve before looking at Angelo. "I haven't seen them but I'm glad they are watching. I look each time I leave the apartment, but no one seems out of place."

"Good, I'll add two more. Find out as much as you can without making her suspicious."

Nina walked from behind the desk. "I need to get back to the apartment. She's a wreck and didn't want me to leave. After what you told me I'll be more cautious."

Joe jumped up and took her hand. "Promise me you won't go with her."

She kissed him. "I promise."

"Stay at Joe's apartment tonight."

"As long as Monique's in Rome I need to be with her. If she leaves, I will."

When Nina entered the apartment, Monique raced to the door.

"He called," Monique said.

"Is he okay? Where is he?"

"Still in Tunis but I told him to go to Athens. I didn't say you suggested it because he has friends near the port of Piraeus. He'll stay at the Hotel Poseidonas for two nights."

"That's even better than Athens."

"I told him I'd arrive in the morning and booked the eight o'clock flight."

Nina frowned. "Are you sure you want to go?"

"He needs my help."

"What will you do? What about your job?"

"I don't care about the job. He'll find a safe place for us. I'm going to the bank to close my account." She walked out the door.

Nina waited five minutes before calling Joe. She turned on the phone speaker and listened to the ring.

"Embassy, Costa."

"It's me, he called."

"What did he say?"

"Tonight he'll be in Piraeus... at the Poseidonas Hotel."

"Good work."

"She's leaving in the morning."

"To meet him?"

"Yes. No matter what's said, she won't listen."

Joe hesitated. "Are you all right?"

"Yes. Don't worry, I won't go with her."

"Okay. Call if anything else happens."

Chapter XIX

IT'S NINA

Colonel Aldo stepped into Angelo's office unannounced.

Angelo leapt to his feet. "I didn't know you were coming."

"I just left a meeting."

Angelo swallowed and held his breath. "About me?"

"No... budget. Any news?"

Angelo motioned to a large chair at the coffee table. "The Americans got Ayisha out of Tunisia, Gustav is talking and Omar should be in Greece this afternoon."

"What about Majid?"

"The old woman is giving us a lot of information. If Omar stays alive he'll talk, but I need your help with Majid."

Aldo stared at him a moment. "What can I do?"

"Will the Tunisian authorities help us get him?"

Aldo rubbed his chin. "They like their status in the international community. If one of their citizens is named as an international drug trafficker, they're not going to be happy."

"Could you speak with one of your Tunisian contacts?"

"Yes. Write what you want and I'll talk with Colonel Fantar."

"Can he be trusted?"

Aldo looked at him and a slight grin appeared. "All my contacts are trustworthy. Years ago he came here for training. We attended the same class. When their government disbanded the secret police he moved to Internal Security. Fantar's quite ambitious and has a large family. His son-in-law is Italian." Aldo glanced around the room. "Why is Omar going to Greece?"

"Our informant recommended it."

Aldo nodded and raised his eyebrows. "Your informant knows what he's doing. Are you going to tell me who he is?"

Angelo widened his eyes. *A request, not an order.* Like Joe, he trusted few, but Colonel Aldo sat at the top of his list of those held in high esteem. *He'll keep Nina's name secret.*

Joe wouldn't be concerned if he told him Nina was the informant. "First may I ask you a question?"

"Sure."

"Do you remember trying to get your wife to marry you?"

"Odd question. Italian women are demanding. I can't count the number of nights I chased her around Rome trying to convince her how important she is to me."

"Then you'll understand, sir. It's Joe's informant."

Aldo tilted his head and paused before speaking. "Joe made the decision to keep the name secret?"

"Yes, sir. He didn't want to lose his future wife."

The colonel glanced at the floor and back to him. "What do you mean?"

"The informant is my wife's cousin, Nina."

Aldo sat up in the chair. "The flight attendant?"

"Yes, sir. Her roommate is French Algerian... she's Omar's girlfriend."

The colonel took a deep breath and blinked several times. "Damn. I understand."

"Joe's worried about her safety."

The colonel nodded. "He did what we all would do, lie to protect her. Is she safe?"

"My men are watching her."

Aldo stood and headed to the door. "If you need more men, call me."

"Sir?"

Aldo stopped and turned. "Don't worry Angelo. Your family secret is safe with me."

Chapter XX

MONIQUE'S TORMENT

The day before Monique's departure from Rome, Omar arrived in the port city of Piraeus. He sat in the only chair in a room at the Poseidonas Hotel. He lifted his shirt and examined the bandage on his side and the gauze wrapped around his midsection. The sound of an AK-47 still rang in his ears. *I'm lucky it didn't rip me open or hit a rib.* He stared at the television, but did not focus on the blank screen.

A blurred recollection of the last two days in Tunis did not help him answer the question stuck in his mind. *Why? Someone set me up to be killed. Who?* Jamal complained that he didn't need help to offload the drugs, and Majid wasted his money sending one of his men on the trips. *Was it him? Or the African, who thinks he's more important because he's close to Majid? The little killer in Italy? What's his name?* He clamped his teeth together as a sharp pain shot across his midsection. When it subsided, he picked up the television remote and adjusted the pillow on the bed.

An hour later, a loud crash jolted him awake. The doorframe splintered and two men in Hellenic Police officer uniforms burst into the room pointing Glock 21 pistols.

"Don't move," an officer shouted.

Omar bolted upright, raised one hand and grimaced in pain as he pressed the other against his side.

A third officer, with two days growth on his face, stepped through the doorway. "If you say one word, I will break your jaw."

Omar's heartbeat raced, and images of being placed against a wall and executed flashed through his mind. *Majid's men in police uniforms. I'm dead.*

The officer closest to him holstered his weapon and pulled him from the bed.

Omar glanced at his bare feet and handcuffed hands as they shoved him out the door. *Why didn't they kill me?*

In the hallway he came face to face with a stocky man in a suit. The man's smile looked more like a smirk.

"Good evening, Mr. Hassan. I am Carabinieri Captain Angelo Randi. We have been looking for you. I'm here with a

European Arrest Warrant out of Italy. A few of my men and I will make sure you remain safe on our short trip to Rome."

A small amount of drugs. I'll be out of jail in a week.

Monique sat beside Yassine on the rear deck of the twenty-five foot boat heading to a rusted freighter. As they approached, the faded name '*Iran Iris*' became clear on the front of the vessel. A steep set of steel stairs hung from the side of the ship. She looked at her high heels and short skirt. Fifteen minutes after she met Yassine, thoughts of Omar raced through her mind. *This makes little sense. He said to meet him in his room at the Poseidonas.*

"Yassine. Why did he leave the hotel?"

"It is safer on the ship with his friends."

She slipped off her heels, glanced at the stairway and the water. *Glad there are no waves.*

At the top of the stairs, a man in a white uniform waited.

The boat eased beside the ship and made contact with the platform at the base of the stairs. Yassine picked up her suitcase and motioned her toward the tiny landing below the bottom step. She tugged her skirt down and took his hand to steady herself. As she climbed the stairs she glanced at the hand holding her purse and the one gripping the handrail. Behind and below her, Yassine's head was even with her feet. *Get a good look little man. It's as close as you'll ever get.*

When she reached the deck, the man in white held out his hand and helped her from the stairway. Yassine set her bag on the deck.

"Good morning, madam. I am Lieutenant Namood Darzi, the ship's engineer. Omar is waiting."

Finally. She smiled at Namood, pulled her heels from her purse and extended the handle of her suitcase.

"Don't worry about your bag," Namood said. "Someone will bring it to you. It's best if you do not wear high heels. We must go up steep stairs."

Monique returned the shoes to her purse. They entered a steel framed doorway and Namood pointed to stairs. At the top, he led her through passageways to a cabin door and opened it. When she stepped inside, he shoved her toward the bed and pulled handcuffs from his pocket.

Her face contorted, eyes locked on the set of restraints. She raised her hands and froze. "What are you doing? Where's Omar? You said he's here and waiting for me."

The first thing to enter her mind was to stop him. She tightened her muscles and closed her fists. Her heart raced as he closed in on her. She thrust her hands against his chest to shove him aside. Namood grabbed an arm when she made contact and slapped her, knocking her onto the bed. He held her against the mattress and handcuffed one of her hands to the steel frame. Without saying a word, he snatched the purse from her hands, and ripped off her blouse. He stepped back, grinned and walked out, slamming the door.

Monique scanned the cabin and focused on a closed porthole five feet from the bed. *Why are they doing this?* She yanked on the handcuff, causing the metal to dig into her wrist. With her free hand she pressed the trembling fingers of her shackled hand together and attempted to slip from the restraint. The steel cut deeper into her wrist. *Where is Omar?* She froze. *Someone planned this... he's not here.*

The ship shuddered and the sound of steel clanging against steel interrupted her thoughts. *The anchor! Oh my God, we're leaving port.* Monique pulled the sheet from the bed and wrapped it around her body. "Help! Please, someone help me!" A sense of hopelessness overcame her and tears ran across her cheeks. She buried her face in the small pillow.

Over the next two hours, Monique lost track of time as she slipped between outright panic and light sleep. The cabin door swung open and a fat officer, in a sweat stained white uniform, threw her suitcase and purse into a corner. "I'm Captain Jamal Jalili. Your phone rang... I threw it overboard." He smiled, removed his belt and folded it in half. "Give me the sheet."

Her heart pounded and tears filled her eyes. "No! Please." She pulled the sheet tight against her body.

He swung the wide belt and struck her upper arm.

She screamed.

"The sheet," Jamal said.

Monique looked at the welt on her arm and glared at him. *This pig can't be the ship's captain.* "No! Leave me alone."

The pig swung a second time, striking the side of her exposed thigh.

Her free hand pressed against the red mark rising on her leg and she sobbed.

Jamal yanked the sheet from her and shoved her head to the mattress. He clamped a hand around the waistband of her skirt and ripped it. "You're a slave now. You will do as I say or try to swim across the Mediterranean."

"Where's Omar?"

"Forget him. You now belong to me. Take off your dress."

She pulled her torn skirt together. Every muscle in her body stiffened.

Jamal removed a knife from his pocket and opened the blade. "Do not fight. The blade is razor sharp. If I slip, you may bleed to death. The ship has no doctor." As he pulled the waistband away from her body, he slit the skirt to the hem. With one quick pull, he yanked it from her and threw it on the floor.

She slid as far back as possible, pressing herself against the bulkhead, closed her eyes and whimpered.

Chapter XXI

THE SHOOTING

After Monique left for Greece, Joe and Nina spent the morning together at his apartment. At two in the afternoon Joe suggested she pack a suitcase and stay with him until the investigation was completed and everyone arrested. *As long as Majid's free, she's in danger.*

They left the apartment and walked through the busy streets.

Joe squeezed her hand. "Angelo is on his way back to Italy with Omar. Monique will call soon."

Nina looked at her watch. "Greece is an hour ahead of us. I'm worried. She arrived at nine our time and it wouldn't take more than an hour to get to Piraeus. She should have called by now."

"If she went to the hotel they'd tell her the police arrested him. Maybe she's contacting them. Did you try to call her?"

Nina stopped. "Yes. Every call went to her voice mail. When Angelo returns, will you ask him to check with the police in Piraeus?"

"I will. Come. Let's pick up your clothes and get back to my apartment."

While they walked Joe held Nina's hand and spent a few seconds studying each person they passed. Although he knew most of the men in the Fugitive Task Force, he recognized no one.

Ten feet past the door to her building, two men leaned against a Fiat. Lowering his head to her, he whispered. "Those men may be two of our friends."

"Friends?" Nina asked.

"Carabinieri."

"They aren't dressed like police officers."

Joe smiled. "That's the idea. Angelo assigned five of them to keep you safe and I'm guessing about those two."

As they approached the door, Joe focused on a motorcycle parked along the curb fifty feet past the entrance.

The man on the bike looked in their direction, put on his full face-shield helmet and started the motor. *He's staring at us and not checking the street.*

Had the man taken his eyes off them, Joe may have ignored him, at least until the engine cranked to full throttle and the bike raced toward them. He tightened the grip on her hand.

The driver pulled a pistol from his jacket pocket.

"Get down!" Joe grabbed Nina, shoved her to the sidewalk and dropped to one knee. His hunch was correct. The men near the Fiat pulled Beretta semiautomatic pistols. One officer stepped into the street, the other to the sidewalk.

Joe slid his Glock from his back waistband and raised it. One Carabiniere stood between him and the man speeding toward them. *No clear shot.* He lowered the pistol and positioned his body between the threat and Nina.

The man on the motorcycle fired two shots and hit the officer standing in the street. He swung the pistol toward the man in front of Joe and fired three times as the officer aimed his weapon.

Joe felt a sharp pain on the inside of his left forearm and leaned toward the ground.

Nina scrambled to her knees. "What's wrong?" she screamed pulling on his shirt.

Joe pushed her to the pavement. The sound of rapid shots from an assault rifle, drew his attention to the street. An officer holding a Spectre M4 submachine gun ran to his side, pointed the gun down the street and motioned to the door leading inside the building.

Joe pulled Nina to her feet. "Go!" He pushed her to the door.

Once inside, he raised his arm.

"God! Your arm... it's bleeding!" Nina stared at the torn flesh, gasped, and covered her mouth. "You need a doctor!" She burst into tears.

Joe ripped off his shirt and wrapped it around his arm. "Stay here."

"No!"

He held his hand in front of her. "Please, I need to look." He opened the door and made eye contact with the officer carrying the submachine gun.

"It's safe now," the man said.

Two officers kneeled in the street beside the injured Carabiniere. A few feet away, a bloody body lay beside an overturned motorcycle.

Joe adjusted the pistol in his waistband and looked back into the doorway. "It's over, you can come out."

Nina stepped beside him and pulled her cell phone from her pocket. "I'll call an ambulance."

Joe held up his hand. "Not yet."

"Why did he try to kill you?"

"Not me." He pressed his lips together and raised his eyebrows. "He aimed at you."

"No, please. I can't..."

An officer standing near the injured Carabiniere, walked to him. "Inspector Costa, I'm Claudio. We called an ambulance. They'll take you and our man to Gemelli Hospital. Colonel Aldo will meet you."

Joe tightened the bloody shirt wrapped around his arm. "They can take him. I'll be fine, I'll go later."

The officer shook his head. "It's best if you and the girl leave before the news media arrive. The colonel told me to tell you not to argue, he wants to talk to you before he calls the embassy."

Nina latched onto his uninjured arm. "I'm going with you."

Chapter XXII

RESOLUTION

Majid dropped two documents on his desk and looked at his watch. *Seven thirty. I stayed too late.*

A knock on the door startled him and Kojo walked into the room. "Sir, Colonel Ali Fantar is here."

Majid frowned. *The colonel always sends his men. It must be important.* "Send him in."

Ali, in a tailored dark suit, came onto the office with a smile. He motioned with his right hand. "Sorry to bother you, Majid."

Majid's eyes locked on the colonel's missing middle finger. *They died taking it from him.*

Ali pointed to Kojo. "If the big man wants a better job, send him to me."

"You can't pay him enough." Majid stepped from behind his desk. "Leave us, Kojo."

He left the room and closed the door.

"Glad to see you, colonel. What can I do for you?"

"I'm sorry to bother you at night."

Majid nodded. "I'm always prepared to help the government. Would you like something to drink?" He pointed to a chair and sat on the couch.

"No, thank you."

"What brings you to my humble company?"

Ali tilted his head and pressed his lips together. "We have two bodies at our headquarters. You might know them or may at least recognize them."

Majid raised his eyebrows. "I doubt I can help you. I don't get out as much as I did years ago. Kojo knows all my employees and friends. Would you like him to go with you?"

"It's best if you come to see what has happened. Someone carved your name into one man's chest."

Majid wasn't surprised at Ali's bluntness. His words were meant to elicit a reaction. *Does he have information about the Iran Iris and the shipment?* He wouldn't give his old adversary satisfaction and eased from the couch. "Let me get my jacket... my driver will follow you."

Ali stood. "We're parked out front."

Lieutenant Namood and the helmsman stood on the bridge of the *Iran Iris*. Jamal Jalili sat in the captain's chair reading a book.

Namood raised his binoculars. "Italian Coast Guard, they'll pass to our stern."

Jamal looked over his shoulder. "Ahead full... keep your eyes on them."

Namood focused on the Italian cutter for two minutes. He lowered the field glasses. "They turned and increased speed."

A seaman scurried onto the bridge. "The Italians are telling us to stop and prepare to be boarded."

Jamal turned his chair towards the man. "Did you answer them?"

"No, sir."

"Don't respond."

The seaman spun around and ran.

"What should we do?" Namood asked.

The captain glared at him. "Nothing. Continue to watch them."

He raised the binoculars. "They'll soon be off our stern, port side."

"How far are they?" Jamal asked.

"One kilometer."

"Starboard twenty degrees," Jamal yelled at the helmsman. "Tell me if they turn."

Namood pressed the field glasses to his eyes as the Italian cutter closed in on the *Iran Iris*. "Five hundred meters and they are turning," he shouted and lowered the field glasses. "They're manning their deck gun!"

The seaman leaned his head through the doorway. "We are to stop or they will disable us."

The field glasses dropped from Namood's hand and bounced on the deck. "If they hit the explosives we'll be killed."

Jamal turned to the seaman. "Tell them we'll comply. All stop."

Namood's trembling hand picked up the binoculars. He turned to the captain. "We'll go to jail."

"Shut up!" Jamal yelled. "We're moving cargo from one port to another. We load what is on the manifest."

He took a deep breath. "What about the girl?"

"There is no reason to enter a cabin. Lower the accommodation ladder and quit shaking. Italy has no authority in these waters."

Coast Guard Lieutenant Falco, followed by three guardsmen carrying Fabarn FP6 shotguns, stepped from the ladder onto the deck.

"Welcome aboard Lieutenant, I'm Namood Darsi, the ship's engineer."

"I'm Lieutenant Falco." He spotted the captain rushing toward him.

"I'm Captain Jalili. What are you doing? You can't threaten to shoot at me and stop my ship!"

Falco stared at the fat officer. *Typical. He thinks he's the master of something the size of the Costa Concordia.* "We are sorry for the inconvenience, Captain. The World Health Organization reported six cases of cholera on a vessel coming out of the Port of Zadar, Croatia. Your ship recently docked there."

"No member of my crew is sick."

"Good." Falco smiled and nodded. "We'll perform a quick safety inspection and you can be on your way."

Jamal stepped close to Falco. "Safety inspection!" Jamal yelled. "You have no authority outside your jurisdiction. We're not in..."

"Italian waters?" Falco removed a handheld GPS from his pocket and tapped the screen. "Eight hundred meters inside the territorial jurisdiction... off the Cape of Otranto." He smiled and handed the GPS to Jamal.

Jamal's face turned red and contorted in anger as he looked at the GPS. "You forced my vessel into your waters?"

"You are mistaken, Captain. We gave no orders for you to change course. To do so must have been your decision. If you wish, I can arrange for you to listen to recordings of our communications and view the radar images. But, that will take two or more hours. The sooner I start my inspection, the less time I will detain you. Please tell the crew gather on the stern. You may remain on the bridge."

Falco took the GPS and turned to his men. "Carmine and Mimo, wait for the crew on the stern. Peppe, make sure the cabin passageways are clear." He stepped past Jamal.

"Excuse me, captain," and walked toward the back of the vessel with the two men. *Fat man will suffer a heart attack when we tell him his run-down freighter is headed to an Italian port.*

Peppe paused in a passageway to check a fire hose. He hummed his favorite tune by Laura Pausini and continued along his route. As he approached the door marked 'CAPTAIN', he stopped and quit humming. *Sounds like a woman sobbing.* He squinted and looked in both directions. Unsure of himself, he shrugged and continued past the Captain's door. As he approached the next cabin, a woman moaned.

He walked to the cabin and opened the door. A woman, half covered with a blood-stained sheet, lay face down on the bed, crying. He jumped back, slammed the door and scrambled down the corridor.

When he reached the main deck, he ran to the stern.

"That was quick... you finished?" Falco asked. He stared at Peppe and frowned. "What's the matter? What happened?"

"Sir. A lady is bleeding."

"What? Where?"

Peppe caught his breath. "The cabin next to the captain's quarters."

Falco looked at the crew and his two men gathered on the stern deck. "Mimo, go to the bridge and keep your eyes on the captain and engineer. Carmine, stay with these men." He turned to Peppe. "Show me."

Peppe stopped in front of the cabin door and pointed.

Falco turned the handle, shoved the door open, and froze.

A woman lying on the bed turned to him. He clamped his teeth together and cringed at her blackened eye, bruised cheek, and handcuffed blood crusted wrist. *Once beautiful, but it's hard to tell now.*

Her eyes widened. She scooted into a corner and pulled the sheet over her upper body.

"My God... get bolt cutters and call for more men! Tell Mimo and Carmine what we found. Don't let the crew, including the officers, hear what you say."

Peppe raced from the room.

Falco stepped to the bed and tightened his jaw when he got a close look at the woman. *She's shaking... frightened. What the hell happened to her?* He kneeled beside the bed and kept his hands at his side. "Do you speak Italian?"

She nodded.

"Don't be scared. No one is here to harm you."

She pressed the sheet to her body and eyed his uniform.

"Where are your clothes?"

"I don't know," she mumbled through swollen lips.

He pulled open drawers until he found a clean sheet and held it to her. "Put the dirty sheet on the floor."

Her face contorted, and she pressed the blood-stained linen against her chest.

Falco unfolded the sheet and placed it next to her. "I'll turn around, cover yourself with the clean one." He turned and waited.

"Okay," she said.

He squatted beside the bed. "Try not to move. We'll help you."

She stared at his uniform. "Who are you?"

"Italian Coast Guard. I'm Lieutenant Falco. Who did this to you?"

The woman lowered her head, sobbed, and struggled to catch her breath. "The captain and another man named Namood."

"How did you get here?"

"I came to meet a friend, and they kidnapped me."

"Are you an Italian citizen?"

"No, French, but I live and work in Rome."

"What's your name?"

"Monique LaCroix."

Peppe scurried into the room holding three-foot long bolt cutters.

"Be careful. Cut the handcuff at her wrist," Falco ordered.

The young man cut the cuff, and Falco held out his hand. "Can you walk?"

"Yes."

He glanced at Peppe. "The captain and crew?"

"No one will argue with our shotguns. The engineer is with Mimo and the captain."

"Good work. We'll be taking these bastards to Brandisi."

Chapter XXIII

ALIVE AND SAFE

Two Alfa Romeo's pulled to the front of Gemelli Hospital on the campus of the Catholic University of the Sacred Heart in Rome. The drivers remained in the cars.

Three Carabinieri, in dark tactical uniforms, exited the second Alfa. Each carried a Spectre M4 submachine gun. One moved to the entrance and two secured the first car.

Angelo, in a black suit, stepped from the right front door and opened the rear door for Nina. Joe, his left arm in a sling, carried his suit jacket, got out behind her, and straightened his tie. Nina took the jacket and draped it over his shoulders.

"Thank you." He kissed her on the cheek. "This morning I considered cutting the sleeve off, but it's a five hundred and fifty euro suit."

Two officers walked beside them as they headed to the entrance.

Angelo led the group to a bank of elevators and when they reached the third floor, he allowed one officer to lead. The group walked to a large waiting room.

Nina glanced around the room, turned to Joe and raised her eyebrows.

Joe leaned to her. "Are you sure you want to see her?"

"Yes. She needs to know her life has changed."

"It's not your fault, she wouldn't listen."

"What will happen to her?" she asked Angelo.

"That depends. If she agrees to testify the government will not charge her with a crime." His cell phone rang, and he left the room.

"Monique's lucky," Joe said.

Nina frowned. "Why do you say that?"

"Because she's alive and may be given an opportunity for a better life."

Nina focused on the floor and took a deep breath. "I hope so. No one should have to face what she did."

Angelo returned with a smile on his face. "Colonel Aldo called."

"Everything okay?" Joe asked.

"He wants us in his office at ten tomorrow morning. Nina also needs to come."

"Why me?"

"I don't know. You played a big part in this case, it must be important." He looked at Joe. "He went to Tunis to identify Majid. Someone cut him into pieces, so I should say to identify his body, after the Tunisians put it back together."

Joe scooted forward in his chair. "Who killed him?"

Angelo shrugged and rolled his eyes. "An investigator said thieves robbed him and he fought for his life."

"Convenient."

"It's odd. Aldo said a police colonel and government officials now have control of his business and property." He held a hand to Nina. "Ready?"

"Yes." She stood, adjusted the one carat pear shaped diamond ring on her finger, and looked at Joe. "Don't tell her I'll be moving in with you."

He nodded, and they followed Angelo to a door.

"Both of you go. I'll talk to her later," Angelo said.

Nina and Joe strolled into the room. It took a moment for them to adjust to the dim light.

Monique's eyes remained closed, a bandage covered one side of her face. Blood stained thick gauze circled one of her wrists. Two IV bags, connected to needles in her arm, hung beside the bed.

Nina's eyes widened. *My God. They beat her.*

Monique opened her eyes, began to cry, and fought to catch her breath. She grabbed Nina's hand.

"You're safe. Everything will be okay now," said Nina.

Her fingers touched Nina's ring, and she looked at it. "You got married after I left?"

"No, engaged." She motioned Joe closer to the bed. "This is my fiancé, Joe."

"Hi, Monique. Talk with Nina. I'll wait in the hall."

She sat on the edge of the bed and held Monique's hand. "I wish you had listened and not gone to meet Omar."

"No one could have stopped me."

This time pay attention. "Do whatever the police say. Find a new life... forget Omar."

Monique sobbed and squeezed her hand. "I loved him... I didn't realize what kind of man he was."

Nina"s brow furrowed. *Sure you didn't.* "Those people have no respect for women or life. Look at what they did to you."

Monique wiped her tears. "You're right. They planned everything before I left Rome. The man that met me at the airport said Omar was hiding on a ship. He lied, but I didn't realize it. I still don't know where he is."

Nina handed her another tissue and rubbed her arm. "Soon you'll get out of the hospital and start a new life. I'm leaving for a month and will be moving. Later you'll meet Carabinieri Captain, Angelo Randi. I asked him to help you find a new apartment. He'll talk to you about Omar and Majid. You need to help him with the investigation."

Monique's eyes widened. "Where's Omar?"

"He's in jail. Someone in Tunisia murdered Majid before they could arrest him."

"I didn't want to see Omar go to jail, but at least he's still alive. Tell Captain Randi I'll help him."

"Good."

For the next thirty minutes they spoke of what would happen in the months to come.

Nina kissed Monique's cheek. "When I return I'll call you." She left the room.

Chapter XXIV

YOUR PLACE IS HERE

Joe and Nina held hands and walked along the corridor to Colonel Aldo's office. Nina tugged Joe's hand and stopped. "Are you hiding something from me? What's this about?"

Joe raised his eyebrows and shrugged. "I don't know. I'm as curious as you."

"Why does he want me here?"

"Like Angelo said, you helped us close this case. He may have a letter thanking you for what you did. If not, I have no idea."

"Did he say anything more to you?"

"No. We're both in the dark. Whatever it is, we'll be surprised." *The colonel wants to surprise her.*

They stepped into the office and stopped near the door.

Colonel Aldo, Angelo, his wife Sofia, and Mia stood in the center of the room talking. They quit speaking and turned toward the door.

Joe squeezed Nina's hand and whispered. "They're here for you."

"Come in, please," said Aldo.

Sofia and Mia rushed to Nina, hugged her and kissed her cheek.

"Show us the ring," Sofia said.

Nina grinned and held out her left hand, the pear shaped diamond sparkled in the light.

Joe approached Colonel Aldo. "Good morning, sir."

"Glad you could come."

"I didn't think I had a choice."

"True." Angelo said.

Aldo moved to the front of his desk and looked at the three women. "Everyone, I have an important announcement."

Joe and Nina joined Angelo, standing between Sofia and Mia.

Aldo took a moment to glance at each person. "For the past two months I've investigated a matter I consider important." He looked at Joe. "The investigation concerns you, Inspector Costa."

"Me?" He looked at Angelo, rigid and expressionless between the two women, and turned back to the colonel. "Did I do something wrong?"

"No," Aldo said. "Not you. It concerns your family in Italy and the United States." He turned to his desk and picked up multiple pages stapled together. He held them up for everyone to see an official Carabinieri investigation report. "One year after your birth, your father, Amadeo Costa, went before American immigration officials and swore he intended to renounce his Italian citizenship." Aldo tapped the papers. "A copy of the form with his signature is attached."

Joe glanced at Nina and back to Aldo. "I can explain. That was so he could become an American citizen."

Aldo raised a hand. "Not now. If you wish to explain in a few moments, you may. Four years later he became a citizen of the United States. The document isn't so important, the dates when this occurred are significant." He set the report on the desk and picked up a large envelope. "Inspector Costa. Have you done anything similar to what your father did? I mean, at any time during your life, did you declare you intended to renounce your citizenship?"

"No, sir." Joe glanced at Angelo and raised his eyebrows.

"Good. Since your date of birth is before your father renounced his Italian citizenship, I took it upon myself," he reached into the envelope and removed a paper, "to complete the process of reinstating your Italian citizenship. It is registered in Campania, in the commune of Giffoni Valle Piana, where your family lives." He handed the document to Joe.

Joe and Nina were the only two not smiling. Stunned, they studied the paper and the official seal at the bottom.

Joe read aloud. "Certificate of Citizenship. This official record certifies that Joseph Anthony Costa is an Italian citizen. Rome, 14 May 2015."

Everyone applauded. Angelo stepped in front of Joe and held out his hand. "Congratulations. You always said you were Italian, now it's official."

Aldo pulled an Italian passport from the envelope. "Here is your passport, you need to sign it and a few documents. A friend at the embassy got the photo from your file."

Joe took the passport. "Thank you, sir."

Aldo slapped him on the side of his shoulder. "If you wish to spend the remaining years of your career in Rome, I'll make it happen. I'm sure your Department of Justice will agree."

"What if they don't?" Joe asked.

Aldo raised both hands. "I can find someone who will explain the importance of Italian-American law enforcement cooperation. If they disagree, you can retire and work for me."

Nina pressed herself against him. "I'll go wherever you want, but it would be nice to stay here."

"Angelo told me Nina's favorite restaurant is the Target near Piazza Repubblica," Aldo said. "I arranged for a large table to be waiting for us at eight tonight. We will toast her for the help she provided us. Without her quick thinking, Omar Hassan would still be a free man and more drugs would flow into Italy."

Sofia tugged on Angelo's sleeve. "My cousin helped you with the investigation?"

"Yes. I'll tell you about it later."

After everyone congratulated Joe he approached Aldo with his hand extended. "Sir, thank you for what you've done. Nina and I are looking forward to tonight."

"Tonight we celebrate. We'll talk again in a few days. Angelo has the papers you need to sign."

Joe caught up with Angelo in the hall. The women walked in front of them. "Did the colonel tell you about this?"

"Of course."

"And you kept it secret?"

"I had to."

"Why?"

Angelo grinned. "I wanted to see your expression."

Chapter XXV

A RAY OF SUNSHINE

Gustav wasn't a happy man. *I gave them information. Why am I still here?*

He had told the captain everything he knew and Randi promised to move him to a new jail when the colonel signed the papers. The authorities now said the colonel had sent the transfer papers to a general for approval. *How long can that take?*

Gustav paced beside the rust pitted bars of the filthy six by ten feet windowless cell. The uneven concrete floor and stained walls revealed its decades of use. He glanced at Omar sleeping on the upper bunk. Prior to being moved into this cell he had never met the man who now spent most of his days sobbing, moaning, and asking to see his girlfriend.

In the center of the ceiling a single bulb glowed inside a thick plastic fixture recessed in the cement.

He walked to the center of the room and looked up at an open four-inch wide pipe protruding from the concrete. A drop of water fell from the mold at the end of the pipe and landed on his forehead. He squinted and focused on a distant, weak glimmer of sunlight barely visible at the other end of the pipe.

THE END